FIGHTING 'round the CHRISTMAS TREE

NIKKI ASH

'Twas the night before Christmas...

To my mom,

who always made sure every Christmas was filled with

love and laughter and family.

Cooper

"NO, ELSA! STAY AWAY FROM THE DAMN TREE." FOR THE millionth time since we got this damn dog I'm shooing her away from the Christmas tree. The Christmas tree that Liz insists we put up every year the day before Thanksgiving so we can decorate it on Thanksgiving. The Christmas tree she says she needs to look at during the month of December because it's so pretty and is filled with so many memories. The same Christmas tree that never has a single damn present under it because every year we leave the day after the kids get out of school for winter break and head to Breckenridge for two weeks to celebrate Christmas with our family and friends. The Christmas tree she makes me take down before we leave, so it doesn't die while we're away because God forbid the poor tree be brown and dead when we return home. Are you doing the math, here? Yep! That means this damn Christmas tree is up for two damn weeks! During which time, I spend countless hours yelling at the goddamn dog to stay away from the goddamn tree.

"Cooper, honey. Can you please stop yelling at the poor dog? You know she's getting older. She's just trying to find a comfy spot to lie down." Are you listening to this crap? The dog has been rolling around under the tree, knocking the ornaments off the branches since the first Christmas we got her. At least she'll be staying at the dog daycare while we're away this year.

"Okay, babe. I need to run to the gym. With Mason winning his fight a few weeks ago, the women have been stalking the gym to check him out and take pictures, and I need to check on a few things before we leave for Colorado."

Mason Street joined my gym a little over two years ago. He was eighteen—broke and lost—living on the streets, but a damn good fighter, and with Kaden's guidance he's soaring to the top, fast. The kid is making a name for himself. A few months after he started training, Ashley found out he was sleeping on benches in various parks and insisted he move in with them.

I walk out of the living room and find Liz standing in the foyer sifting through the mail she must have brought in. Dressed in an off-the-shoulder cream colored sweater, dark skinny jeans, and those fluffy expensive boots she loves, my wife of almost fourteen years still makes casual look sexy as fuck. Coming up behind her, I wrap my arms around her waist and give her bare shoulder a kiss.

"I thought you were leaving." She giggles as I trail wet kisses up the side of her neck, ending at her ear. She tilts her head to the side to give me access and I growl into her ear, making her laugh harder. I will never get enough of this woman.

"I was leaving...until I saw your sexy ass in those tight—" My words are cut off when I see the envelope she's holding in her hand. "What's that?" Reluctantly peeling myself off her, I go to grab the envelope from out of her hands, but she turns around quickly, preventing me from getting it. "Is that what I think it is?"

"Cooper, calm down. You knew this was a possibility." She uses her mom voice on me and I know I'm about to be pissed.

"No, I'm pretty sure I knew my answer was no. ...let me rephrase...Hell. No. Let me see it."

"Not until you calm down." She quirks her brow at me, and normally it would stop me in my tracks and make me rethink whatever it is I'm about to do, but right now I'm on a damn mission, and no look is going to deter me.

"Liz, let me see the damn envelope." Before I can grab it from her, there's a crashing sound from the living room. *Damn dog!* "Just great! Elsa! Get away from the tree!" I bark out. "How many more days until we take this damn tree down?"

"Real nice, Cooper." Liz glares at me. "Why don't we just call you the Grinch?" She huffs, throwing her arms in the air and stomping out of the room. Fabulous! I should have just focused on getting her undressed.

"Was that a crashing sound I heard?" Nathan, our twelve-year-old son, comes out of the kitchen with a sandwich in one hand and a glass of milk in the other.

"Yeah, the dog is rolling under the tree again. God knows how many ornaments are broken this time." I watch him shove the sandwich into his mouth, crumbs falling to the floor. "And hey, how about grabbing a plate instead leaving a trail of breadcrumbs behind you."

Nathan rolls his eyes in typical pre-teen fashion. "Dad, the dog does this every year. Are you really pissed over a couple broken ornaments?" Nathan walks back into the kitchen and grabs a plate. "Happy now?" He sits at the island and continues eating his sandwich.

"Very, and how about you watch your mouth. Did you see your mom come through here?" I could have sworn she came this way.

"Yeah, she threw the mail on the counter and kept going. She didn't look very happy. What'd you do this time?" He laughs, and if I was a tad bit less mature, I'd accidentally spill his milk all over him.

Snatching up the mail, I search for the envelope, but it's not there. She must have taken it with her. "Who said I did anything? And why is it always my fault when your mom is upset?"

"Probably because you're usually the person to upset her," Bella chimes in. She's dressed in her workout clothes with a *Cooper's Fight Club* hoodie on. She swings the fridge door open and grabs a bottle of water and an apple, then sits down at the breakfast bar next to her brother. It's hard to believe my little princess is going to be graduating from high school in a few short months. It feels like yesterday I was running into her at the grocery store. I would give anything for time to stop. Hell, maybe if it could even just slow down, that would be great.

"Dad, are you okay?" Bella looks at me like I'm going crazy.

"Yeah, Princess, I'm okay." My voice breaks from the heavy emotions I'm suddenly feeling. Without giving it a second thought, I'm wrapping my arms around my daughter and hugging her tight.

"Dad, seriously, what's wrong?"

"Can't a dad hug his little girl?" *And never let her go...*

"You can hug me, Daddy!" Lilly, our youngest at ten years old, comes barreling into the kitchen attaching herself to my side.

"Thank you, Lil." I pick her up, making her long legs dangle off the ground and give her a bear hug, squeezing her tight until she starts squealing. "Daddy! You're going to squeeze all the love outta me, silly!" These kids need to stop growing up.

I set her down and turn toward Bella. "Hey Bella, I was thinking this trip to Breckenridge, you and I can spend some time together."

"What's going on, Dad?" She looks at me accusingly as she takes a bite of her apple and pulls her cell phone out of the front of her hoodie.

"Nothing. Can't a dad want to spend time with his eldest child?"

She looks up from her phone and gives me a look that says she thinks I've lost my mind. "He can...I'm sure we'll spend plenty of time together. I need to get going to the gym."

"I'm heading there now if you want to ride together."

Bella opens her mouth but closes it, her eyes squinting at something over my shoulder. Turning around, I spot Liz shaking her head. Damn, I guess it's going to be like that.

"Really? Okay, I guess we're going to have this conversation right here."

"What conversation?" Nathan asks with his mouth full of food. Now he's chowing down on some cookies.

Damn kid never stops eating.

"I need to get to the gym," Bella says, taking another bite of her apple.

"I'll have a conversation, Daddy," Lilly croons sweetly.

"I need to get back to the rec center. I'm meeting Ashley over there to go over a couple things before we all leave for the week." Liz grabs her purse from the counter, attempting to calmly run away.

Running to the doorway, I block the exit. "Hold up." Pointing to the bar stools, I demand, "Everyone sit. Now."

Looking at me like I've lost my mind, everyone sits on a bar stool. I come around to Liz and grab her purse. "Cooper! Give me my purse!" she shrieks.

Ignoring her, I take the large white envelope out, then open it up.

Dear Isabella Cooper,

It is a great pleasure to offer you admission to the University of California for the upcoming

fall semester...

The letter goes on to state she will be receiving a full academic scholarship and the deadline for her to accept or decline. "No." I throw the letter on the kitchen island. "My answer is no."

"Cooper, don't do this," Liz warns.

"What is that?" Bella questions. She gets up and comes around the breakfast bar, picking up the offensive piece of paper. After a few seconds, she gasps. "Oh. My. God! Omigod! Oh my God! I was accepted! Mom, did you see this?" She turns the stupid letter around to show Liz, then after looking at it again, she starts jumping up and down. "I can't believe this! I have to call Tristan and see if he was accepted." She runs over to her mom and hugs her, then grabbing her phone, goes to call her best friend.

"Stop it right there." She turns back around in the doorway. "Didn't you hear me? My answer is no. You aren't going." Bella's head tilts slightly to the side, her hands going to her hips, and in that moment, she looks more like her scary-as-fuck aunt Kayla than her sweet mother. I blame Kayla for her attitude. It was those first four years before I was aware I had a daughter when Kayla helped raise Bella. The woman ruined her for life.

"Seriously?" she says, venom in her voice.

"You aren't going," I insist.

"Cooper." Liz puts her hand on my chest.

"You can't be serious. I didn't even want to go to college. I wanted to fight. But you said I have to go. You said the only way you would support my fighting career is if I go to college. So, I applied to the college I want to go to and I got in just like you wanted, and now you're going to tell me I can't go?"

"I didn't say you can't go to college. I'm just saying you can't go to college in California...or in any other state for that matter." I shrug. "There are plenty of great universities right here in Nevada. Your mother went to one."

"I'm not going to argue with you, Dad. You're being ridiculous. I'm going to the gym." Bella turns her back on me and a few seconds later the front door slams.

"Okay...well that was fun. Mom, can you take me over to the rec center with you? My friend, Colton, is going to meet me there," Nathan says while chewing on a granola bar.

"Have you finished packing for the trip yet? We're leaving Tuesday morning first thing," Liz reminds him.

"All packed," he assures her.

I'm still staring at the front door while everyone goes about their business like my precious daughter didn't just tell me she's about to move away from me to go to college in another state. My world feels like it's caving in and my family is acting like nothing is wrong. Am I the only sane one here?

"Okay. C'mon, Lilly. You can come hang out there with us. I'm only going to be there for a couple hours," Liz says to Lilly. Then she comes over and gives me a chaste kiss on my cheek. "I love you, Coop, but you need to think long and hard about the way you're acting. You're only going to push her away."

They file out, the front door closing once again, and I'm left in the kitchen alone. I can't lose my baby girl. I've only had her in my life for fourteen years. I didn't get her for the first four years, and I need that time to make up for it. My mind starts reeling, my heart racing. She's going to graduate and move to another state. She's going to go to college and meet new people and forget about me and her home. What if she doesn't return? What if she decides to live in California permanently? I can't lose my princess. It feels like I just got her.

Crash!

Motherfucking goddamned dog! "No, Elsa!"

Liz

I'M WORKING ON SOME PAPERWORK FOR ACCOUNTS receivable at the rec center. It's a huge sports complex that provides kids and teens with a safe place to be active after school and on the weekends as well as during the summer. The only time it's closed is for winter break. The center has areas for all different types of sports, such as an area for mixed-martial-arts, an indoor basketball court, an outdoor tennis court, and racquetball courts, as well as a soccer field. There's also a huge trampoline area, and an area for Xbox360 and Wii, which only get used for sports and dancing related games, and only on rainy days. There's also an Olympic-sized pool for swim lessons with two different level diving boards, and we're currently working on opening an area for gymnastics and dance. Lilly loves to do hip-hop dance.

When Cooper, Caleb, Bentley, and Kaden joined forces to create this place, I thought they were in over their heads. *Four men with too much money on their hands* was my initial thought. Their idea stemmed from Marco running the streets when he was younger, and their hearts were in the right place, but I wasn't sure if they could pull it off.

I never should've doubted those men. When they set their minds to something, nothing will stop them. Eight years later, and the recreational center is thriving and has a long wait list. Kids and teens from low income families always get approved first, but everyone is welcome with a membership.

Ashley runs the center and does an amazing job, while I make sure everything money-related is handled—from donations, to paychecks, to making sure memberships fees are paid. All our kids have grown up here. Well, Bella and Tristan are usually at the gym, but the rest of the kids are usually here with us. With Emma, Ashley and Kaden's daughter, getting older and getting more into MMA lately, she's been at the gym more often these days following her older brother and Bella around.

The door to the office opens and Ashley falls into the chair across from my desk with an exasperated sigh. "Thank goodness this place closes in a few hours. I haven't even started packing yet."

"I still need to finish. I went home for lunch thinking I could get some more packing done, but my home turned into a war zone. I ended up leaving without getting anything done."

"Oh no, what happened?"

"Bella got accepted to the University of California," I say with a huge smile, so damn proud of my daughter. She's smart and independent, and she has always been a good kid and now teenager. It's felt like in a way, she and I have grown up together because of me having her at such a young age. She could have fought going to college, but instead she accepted it and is embracing it. Of course, I'll miss her like crazy, but I'm thrilled she wants to spread her wings and fly, even if it is in another state.

"Tristan got his letter as well. I take it Cooper wasn't thrilled."

"Oh, Ashley, you should have seen him. I'm talking veins popping out, fists clenching, eyes going all buggy. He's going to lose it when she actually leaves."

Ashley and I laugh, imagining Cooper's upcoming freak out.

"Have you heard what's happening to Mason?" Ashley asks, changing the subject.

"Sort of. Cooper said he was going to the gym to check on him. Something about girls stalking him and taking photos. What happened?"

"Since he won his fight, the girls have been camped out at the gym wanting a piece of him. It's worse than when Marco gained a fan base. I feel so bad for him."

"Who?" Hayley walks in and sits in the chair next to Ashley, joining in on our conversation.

"Mason. The girls are relentless."

"Ohhh yeah, I just came from the gym. He doesn't appear to be too shaken by all the girls. He's soaking up the attention like a sponge." Hayley shakes her head. "I'm just glad he's keeping Caleb busy. Since he officially retired from the UFC a few months ago, he's been home bored and driving Mackenzie and me nuts! I was about to ship his ass to California to visit Marco. Seeing him at the gym, in his element, is giving me some hope. Maybe he'll get his ass off the couch a few days a week and stop sulking!" We laugh at her, completely understanding where she's coming from.

"Yeah, well, you think he's sulking? You didn't see Cooper this afternoon when Bella told him she's going to college in California and walked out on him, slamming the door. My heart kind of broke for my husband. He's not taking this well at all."

"Is Tristan going to California too?" Hayley asks.

"He sure is," Ashley answers.

"Are you all right with that?" I ask.

"Oh, Liz, our kids have been best friends their entire lives. You know I love Bella like she's my own."

"But," Hayley adds.

"But I was kind of hoping Tristan would use college as a time to find himself. He swears he doesn't want anything more with Bella than their friendship, but I still think in the back of his mind, he's hoping one day a spark will ignite."

"He dates other girls, right?" Hayley asks.

"Yeah, he does, and as much as I wish he was still my baby, I know he's had sex. But the relationships never last long. He always finds a stupid reason to end it or the girl gets jealous of Bella and his friendship. I don't blame Bella at all."

"Oh, I know you don't," I say, and I do know she doesn't blame Bella. We've made sure not to allow anything that happens between our kids come between us. They're young and hormonal.

"Is Bella having sex?" Hayley asks.

"As far as I know, not yet. Her world revolves around fighting. We've had several talks, but she insists she's not ready and when she is, she'll come to me. I can only hope she does."

"Ugh! Can you imagine how crazy Cooper will act when she actually opens her eyes and decides to date?" Ashley snickers.

"Laugh it up. Wait until your two mini-versions of you start to date! Kaden is going to lock their asses up."

"True statement." We all crack up.

There's a knock at the door. "Come in," we yell in unison, making us laugh some more.

"Mom...Oh, hey, Ashley, Hayley." Bella comes inside and leans against the wall in my small office.

"Everything okay, sweetie?"

"I was hoping we could talk." She looks from me to

Hayley and Ashley. The women get it and get up, each of them giving Bella a kiss on her forehead on their way out, quickly congratulating her on getting into college.

Bella closes the door behind her and sits across from me. I take a minute to look at my little girl who has turned into a beautiful young woman right before my eyes. Tears prick my eyes and, before I can stop them, they fall.

"Oh, Mom." Bella jumps out of her seat and into my lap, giving me a hug while almost crushing my legs in the process. I wrap her up in my arms and remember all the years it was just Kayla, Bella, and me against the world.

"I love you, sweet girl."

"Mom, please don't cry. You know I'm not leaving for good, right?"

"Oh, sweetie, I know, and even if you decided to make California your home, I wouldn't stop you. I remember when Kayla and I took off to Las Vegas. Our parents thought we were crazy, but nobody was stopping us. I always thought I would be back after college, but here I am, over eighteen years later and still in Las Vegas."

"You'll visit me, right? And we can talk on the phone every day."

"Of course! And any time you want to come home, you just let us know and a plane ticket will be waiting. I'm so proud of the person you've become, Bella." Tilting her chin up, I look into my daughter's now teary eyes and wipe a falling tear. "You're beautiful on the inside and out. You're smart and determined and you're going to do amazing things. One day you'll be a UFC women's division champion."

"Do you think I'm making a mistake going to California?"

"I can't answer that. Only you know the answer to that question. All I want is for you to be happy."

"Do you think if I go Dad will hate me?"

"I will *never* hate you, Princess." Bella and I look

to the door to find Cooper standing in the doorway. "I didn't mean to intrude. I thought your mom was in here alone. Come here, Bella."

Getting off my lap, Bella runs into her father's arms, the sound of sobs breaking through. "Please don't be mad, Dad."

"I could never hate you or be mad at you, Bella. I know I'm being selfish, but I'm just not ready to let you go yet. The truth is I don't think I'll ever be ready to let you go."

"Mom said she's going to visit me. You can visit me too, you know." She looks up at her father with hopeful eyes.

"Nothing will keep me away. And if you need anything, your mother and I are only a phone call away. But can you do me one favor?"

Bella backs up a little from her dad. "What is it?"

"From now until August, can we pretend like you aren't going anywhere? Can you let me live in denial for a little while longer? Because in my eyes, you're still my little girl."

"Sure, dad. You can live in denial...but only until June."

"What do you mean June? College doesn't start until August."

"I'm guessing you didn't read the entire letter. They also offered me early acceptance if I choose to start this summer, and I think I'm going to."

"Did they offer that to Tristan as well?" Cooper looks from Bella to me, panic evident in his eyes.

"No, but he'll be there in August. I was thinking we could fly out there over spring break to find an apartment. Kaden said it'll be cheaper for us to get a place right off campus. My scholarship covers the cost of the dorm, so my half is taken care of. Tristan got accepted for a partial scholarship, but he has to pay for his own housing. We're going to get a two-bedroom place."

Cooper stares at Bella like she's an alien. "Holy shit, you have this all figured out. Denial...give me denial until spring break then we can look at apartments, okay?"

"Okay, Dad." Bella reaches up and gives her father a kiss on his cheek before walking out of the office.

"Bella," I call out. "Please be home early tonight. You still need to pack and you have one more final on Monday."

"I know, Mom."

Bentley

"CHLOE! FAITH!" I CALL OUT MY DAUGHTERS' NAMES FOR the third time and still get no answer, so I do what any parent would do...I text them...from downstairs.

Group conversation (Family)

Me: Items you need to pack.

shirts

jeans

ski jackets

snow suit

socks

underwear

shoes

phone

iPad

charger

pajamas

toothbrush

hair brush

Chloe: okay

Faith: okay

Kayla: I'll be home in twenty minutes. Love you, baby. <Insert kissy face emoji>

Chloe: Eww! Text that out of the group chat!

Faith: Seriously! Gag!

Perfect! I yell out my daughters' names and get no response, but I send them a damn text and they respond immediately. Not that it should surprise me—my daughters are eleven going on eighteen.

"Hey buddy, you want to help me pack up your stuff?" I wait for Ryan to answer, but he doesn't, and as usual my heart cracks.

I reach for Ryan and his arms lift, letting me know he's okay with me picking him up. I carry him up the stairs to his room and set him down on his bed. Ryan Cruz is four years old and the newest member of our family. Kayla and I didn't plan to expand our family, but when Sheila, a friend of ours who works for the Department of Children and Families, mentioned Ryan while visiting the rec center, my heart broke.

Ryan was born into a broken family. His mom gave birth to him at only fourteen years old. She tried to be a good mom to him, but her parents weren't supportive and made her do it all on her own. When Ryan was two, she couldn't handle it anymore, so she dropped him off at his dad's house and ran away. The police found her dead in an alley a week later—overdose.

Unfortunately, Ryan's biological father wasn't the better option. At eighteen years old, his only purpose in life was to get high and make money. Nobody knows what happened to Ryan, but after a year of living in his father's apartment, a neighbor made a complaint about a child crying.

His father wasn't home, so the police waited for him to return, then arrested him for child neglect and endangerment, along with several other drug charges. Luckily, he signed away his rights and the biological family felt it was best not to adopt him. So, when Sheila brought Ryan up to us, we were able to adopt him without any complications.

We agreed to go meet him, not wanting to commit to anything right away. When we saw Ryan sitting at the table in his foster parents' house, coloring on some paper, he turned to look at us, and my eyes locked with his, and I knew in my heart, he was meant to be our son. It's been six months since Ryan has joined our family, but he hasn't spoken a single word to any of us.

I spoke with his biological grandparents once right after we adopted Ryan, and they said he spoke occasionally when he was with his mother, so we know he's capable. The therapist says he just needs time. She calls it selective mutism. He's capable of talking, but is choosing not to.

It's crazy how without him even saying a word, he has won over every person in this house as well as all our friends and family. We've all been learning sign language the best we can and it helps with communicating with him. He nods and shakes his head, he points to what he wants, and he cries when he's upset. His smile can damn near light up a room, and a few times, when his laughter wasn't silent brought me to tears.

With the girls in school, that leaves Ryan and me to hang out all day since I'm still a stay-at-home dad. We spend many days at the gym hanging with the guys, a lot of time at the parks, the local pools, and museums to socialize. Ryan plays well, but instead of playing with other kids, he chooses to play near them. The therapist says that's normal. He needs to learn to trust those around him.

"Okay, Ry. We need to pack you some warm clothes. In a couple days, you're going to see snow. Have you ever seen snow?" Ryan shakes his head. "Do you know what snow is?" He shakes his head again. "Oh, little man, it's going to be awesome." I pull out my phone and pull up YouTube to find a home video someone made of snow falling, and hand it to him to watch while I grab all the clothes he'll need for our two weeks in Breckenridge.

"Dad!" Chloe yells at the top of her lungs. *Maybe I should ignore her like she ignores me.*

"Dad!" Faith screams out. Seriously? They both ignored me, but they think I'm supposed to acknowledge them when they call out. Two sets of feet come stomping down the hall and stop when they get to Ryan's room.

"Dad, we were calling you," Chloe says, exasperated.

"Oh, sorry. I thought when we screamed out each other's name, we were supposed to stay silent until the person texted the other person." Both girls just look at me dumbfounded, not getting the sarcasm. "Never mind. What's up?"

Chloe and Faith sit on the bed sandwiching Ryan in, giving him hugs and kisses. Before we made the decision to go see Ryan, Kayla and I sat down with the girls to see how they would feel about us possibly adopting again. Chloe thought it was an amazing idea. While she doesn't remember being adopted at only a few months old, we've been completely honest with her. She knows her biological mom overdosed and died, and that Marco, Hayley and Caleb's son, is her biological brother.

When we told them Ryan's mom died, I think it hit home for Chloe. She immediately wanted to make him a part of this family. Faith was just as excited, saying she would love to be an older sister. With her and Chloe only a few months apart they might as well be twins, but technically Chloe is the older one of the two.

"Can we have breakfast for dinner tonight? And can Chloe and I make it?" Since Kayla hates cooking and I stay home with the kids, I'm the one in charge of the cooking. I've been teaching the girls how to cook and bake since they were little. Best decision I ever made. Now that they're getting older, they want to make the meals, which means I get to sit back and enjoy.

"Are you girls done packing?"

"Not yet."

"Almost."

"All right, but after dinner you have to finish." I turn to Ryan. "Hey Ry, do you want waffles for dinner?" Ryan nods his head, a ghost of a smile gracing his face.

"C'mon, Ryan, you can help me put the chocolate chips in." Faith takes Ryan's hand and helps him off the bed, holding his hand while they walk out of the room and downstairs to start dinner. I finish grabbing Ryan's clothes and bring it all downstairs, so I can supervise my little chefs.

On my way to the kitchen, there's a knock on the front door. "Girls, don't turn on the waffle maker until I get in there, please," I yell out, swinging the door open to find Nancy Peterson, also known as my mother-in-law, standing there with a rolling luggage next to her. "What are you doing here?"

She frowns, then smiles wide. It's probably the brightest smile I've ever seen her give me and it almost makes me cringe. When Kayla's father passed away last year from a heart attack, she retired from the firm they were partners in and took off traveling the world. Kayla said she called it reinventing herself.

We've received a few post cards, and Kayla said she's texted and called a few times. Kayla and her mother have never had a good relationship. Kayla moved to Las Vegas with her best friend, Liz, at eighteen and never really looked back. Her mom visited once when Faith was little but was cold the entire time. After that, we would visit every few years, stay at a hotel, and try to get her to get to know her granddaughters, but unfortunately, Kayla's parents weren't the loving or nurturing types.

Kayla's brother on the other hand, is a very hands-on uncle when he visits. He lives in Florida with his wife, Vanessa, and their two children, but visits regularly, as well as video chatting a few times a week.

"Mom?" Kayla comes walking up the sidewalk looking sexy as hell in her tight black pencil skirt, white blouse that I can almost see-through, and her black fuck-me heels that she always wears.

"What are you doing here? I thought you were in Italy, based on your most recent post card."

"I'm here to visit my daughter and her family." Kayla and I exchange a *what the fuck* look with each other. "Are you going to invite me in or are we going to just stand in the doorway all evening?"

"Umm...sure...come on in," Kayla mumbles, grabbing her mom's luggage for her. I open the door wider and let them walk in first, taking the luggage from Kayla. Then I go to the kitchen to make sure the kids haven't burnt the kitchen down.

Chloe is talking on the phone, while Faith is bent down with the mixing bowl in her hands as Ryan dumps the bag of chocolate chips into the bowl, his eyes shining with excitement.

"Marco, please. You have to go to Breckenridge," Chloe whines. "We go every year! And I haven't seen you in months. Please." Chloe pouts. It's been hard for her ever since Marco moved to California. While they're nearly twelve years apart, they're still extremely close. I can't hear what her brother is saying but whatever it is, she isn't happy about it. "Fine! Whatever!" She hangs up the phone clearly upset and about to storm out of the kitchen.

Before I can stop her, she takes off. Unfortunately, she doesn't see Faith and Ryan are in her way. Chloe trips over them by accident, sending the bowl flying out of their hands. The spoon clatters on the floor, and the batter flies across the kitchen. Ryan's eyes widen in horror as he watches it all happen, tears welling up in his eyes.

"Oh my God!" Faith yells, mad that her batter is ruined.

"I didn't mean to!" Chloe shouts back.

Ryan's tears begin falling at the screaming. Kayla sees him upset at the same time I do, and scoops him up into her arms.

"Girls," I say, trying to keep my voice calm. Of course they ignore me, arguing over whose fault it is. Maybe I should fucking text them! "Girls," I try again, a bit louder. I'm still being ignored. Ryan's cries get louder, and immediately both girls go quiet, realizing what their fighting is doing to him.

"Ryan, don't cry," Chloe coos.

"It's okay. We can make new batter," Faith tells him.

Both girls try to comfort him with their words,

telling him it wasn't his fault and apologizing for yelling at each other. Ryan, who has his face nuzzled into the crook of Kayla's neck, peeks out at the girls' soothing voices. Then I remember Kayla's mom is here and look around for her. She probably witnessed that scene, grabbed her luggage, and booked the first flight the hell out of this mad house.

I don't see her at first, but then I spot her on her hands and knees. *What the heck is she doing?* Nancy Peterson, my mother-in-law, is wiping up the battered mess. I almost pull out my phone to video this because Liz would never believe it without the proof. "Nancy, you don't have to do that," I insist.

Kayla looks over at her mom using a wet paper towel on the tile, trying to clean up the mess. She blinks a few times then looks around like she's expecting cameras to pop out and Ashton Kutcher to appear, announcing she's been punked. I cover my mouth to stifle a laugh, until Faith says, "Mom, I thought you once said Grandma would never be caught dead cleaning."

My laugh can no longer be contained. Kayla glares at first but quickly gives up and laughs. We look to her mom and she's sitting up on her heels staring at us. I compose myself and prepare for the wrath of Nancy to come, but instead we get, "Are you enjoying a laugh at my expense?" Standing, she places the bowl on the counter and then...she smiles. Are you keeping count? This woman has smiled twice since she showed up and I'm almost positive it's the most I've ever seen her smile. Her face must be exhausted.

"Mom, are you dying?" Kayla frowns.

"What? Grandma, you're dying?" Faith says, running over to Nancy. She stops before reaching her grandma, unsure of what to do or how to react. Nancy opens her arms, embracing Faith, and then smiles again. *Holy shit! Three times!*

"Oh my God, Mom, you're dying?" Kayla starts to cry, which causes Ryan to start crying again.

I grab Ryan out of her arms telling him it's okay. "Kayla, woman. Can you calm down, please?" I give her a look then glance down at Ryan so she gets it. She takes a deep breath to calm herself.

"Kayla," her mom admonishes, "I am not dying."

"Then why are you here? Cleaning my floor? And hugging Faith?" Kayla asks incredulously.

"Can't a grandmother help clean up a spill and hug her grandchild? Jesus, Kayla, don't upset everyone into thinking I'm dying." She washes her hands in the sink then walks over to me. "Come here, Ryan." Nancy reaches her arms out to take Ryan from me. He doesn't put his arms out, but that doesn't deter her. She puts her hands under his armpits and takes him out of my arms. "I'm your grandma. I know you aren't ready to talk yet, but when you do, you can call me Grandma."

Everyone in the room just stands there in shock. Kayla's eyes meet mine, hers silently asking, "Who is this woman?" I just shrug, having no clue.

"Girls, since Grandma is here and the batter got messed up, why don't we order in?" I suggest.

"Okay," they agree.

"Do the dishes, please," Kayla adds.

Nancy, still holding Ryan, walks out of the kitchen and into the living room. She sits on the couch and continues to talk to him, asking him questions he doesn't answer, but she just keeps talking like it's perfectly normal to have a one-sided conversation with him.

Kayla and I sit on the couch across from them, watching the interaction. Occasionally Ryan will shake his head or nod. Finally, Kayla speaks up. "Mom, why are you here?"

"Kayla, can't a mother visit her daughter, son-in-law, and grandchildren?"

"Yes, she can, but you never have."

"Of course I have."

"Yeah, once. When Faith was a couple months old. What's going on?"

"Well, maybe while I've been away traveling I've realized how much I've missed, and I came here hoping to spend the holidays with my family. Zach mentioned he, Vanessa, and the kids will be meeting you in Breckenridge for a few days after Christmas, so I thought I could join you guys.

Silence.

"Yay! Grandma, are you going to go skiing with us?" Chloe asks.

"Oh, sweetie, Grandma doesn't—" Kayla starts to say, but her mom cuts her off.

"I sure am! Think you can teach me how?"

Now, I'm looking around for the cameras. Clearly, someone is punking us.

"Yes! Faith and I are awesome at skiing and snowboarding! We can teach you."

"Sounds good! So, when do we leave?"

"Tuesday," I say. "So, Chinese or pizza?"

"Chinese," both girls say.

Kayla just shrugs still in shock.

Ryan doesn't say a word.

Nancy simply smiles.

"Chinese it is."

Kayla

WHEN I SAW MY MOM STANDING ON OUR FRONT DOOR STEP, I honestly thought I was hallucinating. It's not a secret our relationship is pretty much nonexistent. For too many years, I lived my life afraid to love. Between getting my heart broken in high school and my parents trying to instill it in my head love isn't real, my poor husband had his work cut out for him when we met, trying to get me to open up. But he never gave up, and once I found out how amazing love could feel, I made the decision to love those who choose to be in my life, and be okay with not having those who choose not to be in my life.

Watching my mom clean up messes, hold Ryan, and eat Chinese with us around the living room coffee table is amazing and scary at the same time. I keep waiting for

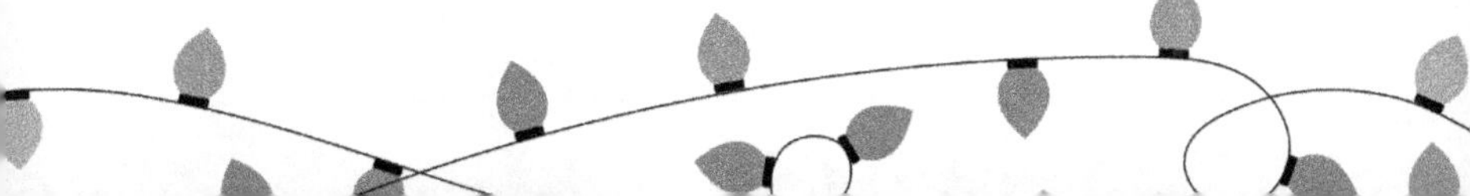

someone to tell me this is all a joke. Years ago, my guard would have been up. I would have told her she's not welcome here, but now, my guard is down, hoping she's for real. If Bentley would have pushed me away at the first sign of issues, we wouldn't have the marriage and life we have today. So, instead of pushing my mom away, I'm going to give her the benefit of the doubt, hoping she doesn't leave again—taking not only my heart but my kids' hearts with her.

After dinner, we all watch a Disney movie, then I set her up in Faith's room—having the girls bunk together—while Bentley gives Ryan a bath. After everyone is down for the night, my mom excuses herself to bed with the excuse of being jetlagged. Bentley says he's going to clean up the dishes from dinner and tells me to go take a shower.

After I'm showered and in bed, I text Liz, telling her all about my evening while Bentley's in the shower.

Liz: She ate Chinese food at the coffee table?

Me: Yes!

Liz: And cleaned up waffle batter from the floor?

Me: That's what I said!

Liz: And kissed and hugged all three kids before they went to sleep?

Me: Yes!!!!!!

Liz: I can't believe it. Maybe Aliens have taken her over her body.

I snort out a laugh.

"What's funny?" Bentley comes out of the bathroom in nothing but a towel, droplets of water trailing down his torso. My mouth goes dry, suddenly feeling parched, needing to lick the beads of water off his abs to hydrate myself. "Kayla?"

"I told Liz about my mom. She doesn't believe me."

"I considered videoing it for her." Bentley drops his towel, grabbing a pair of briefs from the drawer to put on.

"That wouldn't have been weird at all." My phone vibrates a few times, probably Liz wondering why I haven't texted her back, but the only thing on my mind is getting my husband between my legs.

He grabs the towel from the floor and turns around to throw it in the hamper, during which time I pull my pajama shirt up and throw it on the floor, leaving me in only my panties.

"No, it would have been really weird, but at least we would have had..." his words fade off when he sees I'm topless. "Damn, woman." Jumping onto the bed next to me, his mouth goes directly to my nipple, not wasting any time. His hand goes to my other breast, massaging and tweaking the hardened peak.

"Mmm...Bent. That feels good." He continues his onslaught on my breasts. Sucking. Biting. Licking. The perfect balance of pain and pleasure stimulating me all the way to my core.

Taking his dick in my hand, I start to stroke it,

getting it hard. "Baby, I need your dick in my mouth," I moan. He groans in response sucking on my nipple even harder before he lets go of it, backing up.

With his dick in my hand, I pull it toward me, silently telling him to get over here. Sitting up on his knees, Bentley's dick bobs right in my face. I start off stroking it, getting it harder, then cover his entire length with my mouth. Sucking and stroking him turns me on. I can feel myself getting wetter. Bentley pinches and pulls my nipples, while I slurp and suck his dick, his head hitting the back of my throat, turning me on even more. His hand moves to my pussy and his finger stretch me while I continue to suck and fuck him with my mouth.

"Jesus, woman." Bentley backs up, grabbing my legs together, and pushing them up against my chest. In one swift, fluid motion, he thrusts deep into me. A loud moan escapes my lips as he continues to pump in and out of me with a punishing rhythm. My orgasm builds. Suddenly my legs are spread wide and Bentley is covering me, his body flush against mine, his lips brushing mine, then his tongue delves into my mouth, making love to mine while he makes love to me.

In this position, his dick rubs against my clit over and over and over again, bringing me closer and closer to the brink, until we're both taken over the ledge and falling. And holy shit does falling with this man always feel so damn good.

Once we've both cleaned up and lying back in bed with Bentley is spooning me from behind, I broach the subject of my mom. "What do you think about my mom?"

Dusting my hair to the side, Bentley nuzzles his face into the crook of my neck, and peppers me small kisses behind my ear. "I think I don't want to think about your mom after I just nearly fucked you into tomorrow." I laugh and swat at his shoulder. "Okay." He laughs. "I think she wants another chance at being a good mom and grandma. How do you feel about that?"

I think about that for a moment then turn around to face him. "I'm not sure. I spent most of my childhood wishing for her to come around, then most of my adulthood accepting she never would."

"All we can do is give her a chance. Our house in Breckenridge is plenty big enough for all of us and with my parents going away for the holidays, she'll be able to spend time with the kids. But Kayla, if she hurts you, I'm going to send her packing. You've come too far. *We* have come too far, for her to tear you down again. If she resorts back to the way she was, she's gone."

"I agree. I just hope it doesn't come to that. I would love to have a relationship with my mom like I do with yours."

"And I hope it happens, but if it doesn't, she's gone." Cuddling into the crook of Bentley's arm, I lay my cheek down on his chest.

"Thank you, Bent."

"For what, babe?" His arms encircle my .body,

holding me tight against him.

"For always protecting me."

Bentley grabs my chin and tilts my face toward his, then bending his head slightly, he kisses my lips. "I love you, Kayla. You will always come first."

The sunlight comes through the drapes as I hear a whimpering in the baby monitor telling me Ryan is awake. It's the only noise he makes to indicate he's ready to get up for the day. The clock says it's seven in the morning. Bentley is lying next to me—snoring softly—so I turn the monitor off, throw on some pajama pants, and close the door behind me so he can sleep in.

"Morning, Ry," I say once I open the door. He reaches up for me and I take him in my arms giving him a soft kiss to his forehead. After taking him to the bathroom and getting him dressed, we head downstairs for breakfast. Because we're leaving in two days for two weeks, we haven't gone shopping. There's some milk and cereal left for maybe two bowls, but that won't feed all of us.

Just as I'm considering my options, the front door swings open and closed. There's no way Chloe or Faith left this morning. *They better not have!*

"Oh good! You're up." My mom walks into the kitchen with two boxes of donuts and a cup holder full of coffees and milks. "I wasn't sure what everyone eats," she says, her voice sounding unsure, unlike the confident mom I grew up with. She sets the boxes and coffees on the island.

"We aren't picky. Thank you."

She hands me a coffee then turns the box to Ryan so he can pick out a donut. He looks back and forth between us.

"Grandma bought donuts. Pick any one you want." Ryan's eyes go wide. "Go ahead, just point like this." I point to a donut, pick it up, then put it back. Ryan mimics my motion, pointing to a chocolate one with Christmas sprinkles. "Yum! Christmas sprinkles." I pick it up and put it in front of him on a napkin, and my mom puts a glass of milk next to it.

Ryan's hand comes up, his fingers touching his mouth then moving outward—the sign for thank you. It makes me smile seeing him using the sign language we've been teaching him so he can communicate until he's ready to speak.

"You're welcome," I say, while doing the motion in sign language. Then I grab a donut and coffee and join Ryan on the barstool next to him. My mom sits on the other side of him, doing the same.

"Thank you for grabbing breakfast. I imagine today and tomorrow will consist of eating out and ordering in while we get everything ready to leave Tuesday. Bentley didn't want to go grocery shopping and have all the food go bad. He usually cooks the meals.

"So, Bentley is still home with the kids?" my mom asks.

Remembering years ago when we had this

conversation, my initial thought is to defend our life, defend my husband, but this time around her tone isn't judgmental, so I take a mental step back before I jump down her throat.

"Yeah, he loves it. He volunteers at the girls' school a couple days a week and works out at Cooper's gym while they're in school. Since we adopted Ryan six months ago, he's been focusing on him. We're hoping Ryan will be ready to start Kindergarten next August. He also volunteers quite a few hours at the rec center the guys built."

"Oh, yes. I read about it online when it opened. What they're doing is amazing." It's the first time my mom has admitted to knowing what's happening in our lives and it gives me hope.

"It's not just us, though." Bentley walks into the kitchen and straight to me, giving me a peck on my cheek. "Morning, babe." Then he moves to Ryan. "Morning, little man." Ryan gives him a small smile, pointing to the few crumbs left of his donut. "Did you eat that entire donut all by yourself?" Bentley asks dramatically, and Ryan nods.

"What's not just you?" my mom asks Bentley.

"The guys and I had the vision, but our wives helped it come to fruition. Liz does the accounting, Ashley manages the place and runs all the activities, and Kayla and Hayley volunteer their time and donate to the center from their practice."

My mom looks confused. "Practice?"

"Your daughter and Hayley have an extremely successful sports medicine clinic here in Las Vegas. Hayley and two other doctors do the consultations and surgeries, and Kayla runs the physical therapy side of it. She has two PT people who work for her. Sports players come from all over to be seen by them."

The way Bentley explains my career to mom fills my heart with pride. When you live with someone for so many years and are married with children, you don't always remember to compliment each other. You just get so busy with living life. Listening to him, the pride evident in his voice, brings tears to my eyes.

"Kayla, I had no idea. You never told me. I just assumed all these years you were still working at the gym. Honey, I am so proud of you." My mom gets off the stool and walks over to me, enveloping me in a hug. It lasts for several seconds, maybe even a minute before she pulls back, her eyes watery with tears. "Why didn't you tell me?" I don't want to ruin the moment, so I just shrug.

She stares for a moment then sighs. "You didn't tell me because I never asked. I never asked what you were doing or how you were doing. I was so upset about you working for a gym, I pushed you away, making you feel like you couldn't tell me anything. I'm so sorry, Kayla. I know it's going to take time, but I'm hoping you'll let me in and give me another chance."

My throat is clogged with emotion, so I nod in

agreement, and my mom gives me another motherly hug like the ones Bentley's mom gives me all the time.

"Thank you, Kayla. You won't regret it. I promise."

"Oh yeah! Donuts!"

"Heck yeah!"

Chloe and Faith come into the kitchen, each grabbing a donut and stand against the island. "I can't believe you actually bought donuts, Dad," Faith says, stuffing her face.

"I didn't. Your grandma did." Bentley lifts his chin toward my mom.

"Thanks, Grandma!" Chloe's voice is muffled, full of the donut.

"Don't talk with your mouth full of food, please," Bentley admonishes, getting him an eye roll from Chloe.

"Okay, so who's packed and who do we need to get packed?" I ask.

"Kids and I are all packed and the luggage is in the foyer. You're the only one who needs to pack."

"Well then, why don't you girls take Ryan out back to play while I finish packing and then we'll head out and show Grandma around Las Vegas."

"Okay!" both girls exclaim, taking Ryan's hands with theirs out the back door.

Caleb

Me: We'll be in Breckenridge tomorrow. When will you be there?

Marco: I don't think I'll be able to go. Sorry.

Me: Why?

Marco: I need to train.

Me: You just fought less than a month ago and won...I know after a big fight you take a break.

Marco: I need to keep up my momentum.

Me: Marco, you need to join us. Your mom is going to flip her shit.

Marco: She'll be fine.

I slam my phone on the counter and hear the screen shatter into a million pieces. "Fuck!" I'm going to have to go to the store to get a new screen for my phone before we leave.

"What's wrong?" Hayley walks into the kitchen, grabbing a cup of coffee.

"Nothing, Hayles. My screen shattered. I'm going to need to run to the mall and get it replaced."

She sets her coffee down. "I can see that. But my question is, what's wrong? Why did you slam it down hard enough to make it shatter?"

Shit, she saw me slam the phone down. There's no way I'm letting her know Marco isn't planning to come to Breckenridge for Christmas. It'll break her heart. In the two years since Marco moved to California, he's only been back here once, and it was shortly after he left. I'm not sure what happened, but he left without letting us know and hasn't been back since. I've tried to talk to him about it and I know Hayley has as well, but

Marco isn't talking. So instead of getting on him about not coming home, Hayley, Mackenzie, Chloe, and I have been to California several times a year to visit him.

He's also refused every year to go to Breckenridge for Christmas. The first year he refused, Hayley had us all flying out Christmas Eve to spend Christmas with him. Last year, Marco went away with his friends to the Bahamas for Christmas. Hayley was really upset and it just about ruined her Christmas. There's no way he's doing this to her again. If she knew I was arguing with him, she would hide her feelings and tell me to leave him alone.

"Caleb, what's wrong?" she asks again. Her phone buzzes and she quickly grabs it off the counter. After a second, she frowns and puts it back down. I've noticed her doing that several times recently.

"Nothing that can't be fixed. I'm going to run to the mall to get my screen fixed. I should be back in a couple hours." I give her a quick kiss before going to the room to grab my wallet and truck keys.

"Where are you going, Dad?" Mackenzie walks out of her room, her hair looking all crazy from sleeping.

"My screen shattered. I'm going to run to the mall and get it replaced before we leave for Colorado tomorrow."

"Oh! Can I go? I need to get a new jacket for the slopes. Mine is too small."

"How about we buy you one once we're there. You have plenty of jackets to wear for when we get off the plane, right? I'm just going to run in and out."

"Okay." She shrugs and closes the bathroom door.

I don't know how it happened. It's like my mind has a mind of its own, I swear. I'm standing at the airport with a ticket to San Diego International in one hand and my broken phone in the other. I tell myself I can't let Hayley know where I'm going because of the broken phone, but we know that's a crock of shit. I could easily use a payphone or ask someone to borrow theirs, but I choose not to. Calling Hayley means explaining why I'm about to board a plane to San Diego, which will only upset her. I'm hoping by doing this behind her back I'll stop her from being hurt and we'll spend this Christmas as a family.

The woman over the intercom announces my section. I hand her my ticket then head through the gates to board the plane. An hour later, and I'm snagging a cab to Del Mar and thirty minutes later I'm knocking on the door to Marco's apartment, which overlooks the beach. When nobody answers, I curse myself for not getting my phone fixed first, then knock again.

This time, the door opens, only it isn't my son. It's a girl who appears to be the same age as him, standing in the doorway with nothing but a tank top and underwear on, making me look anywhere but at her.

"You aren't Marco," she says.

"No, I'm not. I'm his dad. And you are?" I focus on her face now. She doesn't seem bothered that she's talking to a stranger in her underwear.

"Bianca. You don't look old enough to be his dad."

"Bianca? What are you still doing here?" Marco appears from behind me, dripping in sweat. "Dad?" He looks confused. Then his face morphs into worry. "Are Mom and Mackenzie okay?"

"Yeah, they're fine."

His face turns from worried to annoyed. "Are you here to try to get me to go to Colorado?"

I look from him to Bianca, who is still standing in the doorway in her underwear. "You think you could invite your dad in? Maybe not discuss this in the doorway?"

"Shit, sorry. Come in." Marco reaches over to me giving me a one-armed hug. He smells like sweat and saltwater. He must have been jogging along the beach. I follow them to the living room and sit on the couch. Marco must remember Bianca's still here because he says, "Give me a minute," before he goes to his room with Bianca following behind him. About fifteen minutes later they both emerge. She's finally dressed in more than underwear with a purse slung over her shoulder, and he's freshly showered in basketball shorts and a shirt.

She gives me a soft smile and leaves without Marco saying a word to her. "Girlfriend?" I ask as he sits on the couch across from me.

"Nah."

"Friend?"

"Not really."

"Fuck buddy?"

Marco laughs. "Yeah, I guess you could say that."

"Where's Mathias?" A few years ago, Marco asked me if I would hire someone to dig up information on his biological family. Even though his mom was dead and there wasn't a name listed under father on his birth certificate, he needed to know if he had anyone biologically related to him and his sister Chloe. The detective found one living relative: a sister to his mom, here in California.

I contacted Jennifer without Marco knowing in case she didn't want anything to do with him, but she was elated to find out she had a niece and nephew. Her parents had both passed away and Marco's mom was her only sister. When she got into drugs, she cut ties and had no idea her sister had two children.

Jennifer has a son, Mathias, who's only a couple years older than Marco. After visiting a few times, Marco made the decision to move to California, where he and Mathias share a two-bedroom condo on the beach.

"He's at work until five. I don't think I could ever put on a suit every day and work a nine-to-five job." Marco shakes his head.

"That's because you're a fighter."

We both sit in silence for a few minutes. With Hayley not here to keep the words flowing, we wait for the other to speak.

Marco finally laughs. "Does Mom know you're here?"

I glare. "No, you pissed me off and my screen

shattered. I left to get it fixed and ended up here. She thinks I'm at the mall."

Marco throws his head back in laughter. "Hol-y shit! She's going to kill you."

"No, she's not. You want to know why?"

Marco sobers up. "Why?"

"Because I'm going to return with her sweet little boy." It's Marco's turn to glare. "And once she sees you and hears you'll be gracing us with your presence in Colorado for Christmas, I'll be getting an extra special Christmas gift." I give Marco a taunting wink just to fuck with him.

"Oh, fuck! Really, Dad?"

"Like you don't know anything about getting laid? Your little fuck buddy answered the door in her underwear. Just be glad I didn't have your mom with me."

Marco's eyes widen, thinking about that one.

"I'm not going to Breckenridge."

"Tell me why." I know there's something keeping him away.

"I'm busy here." He doesn't look me in the eyes.

"You're too busy to spend the holidays with the people who love you? That is not the kid your mom and I raised."

Marco sighs then looks me in the eyes, nervously. "Dad, I need to tell you something."

"You can tell me anything. You know that."

Hayley

Me: Did you get your phone fixed?

Me: Hello?

Me: It's been awhile since you left. Are you okay?

Me: Caleb, I'm getting worried.

"MAC, HAVE YOU HEARD FROM YOUR DAD?" I LOOK DOWN at my phone hoping to see a text from Caleb. Every text has turned green indicating his phone is off. I tried to call a couple times and every time it's gone to voicemail. My phone buzzes and I check it, but it's neither of the messages I'm waiting on.

"Nope," she says, looking up from her phone.

"Are you packed? We're leaving first thing in the morning."

"Yeah." She doesn't look up from whoever she's texting with.

"Who are you talking to?"

"Chloe. She said Marco isn't coming to Colorado for Christmas." She rolls her eyes. I didn't know for sure, but I suspected he wouldn't be going. I never came out and asked him, afraid of the response I would get. I kept hoping for a Christmas miracle, but knew it more than likely wouldn't happen.

"Well, maybe we can end our trip a little early and go visit him. He's probably just busy. I can ask Kayla if we can bring Chloe with us."

The front door opens and Caleb walks in. He doesn't shut the door behind him, and then in walks Marco. I run passed my husband and into my son's arms. I haven't seen him in almost six months and I've missed him like crazy.

"Oh, sweetie! You're home." I give him a kiss on his cheek then hug him again. "I missed you so much. I swear you grow taller and bigger every time I see you. Are you coming to Colorado with us?" I don't wait for him to answer before hugging him again.

"I missed you, too, Mom." Marco doesn't move. He lets me hug him and hugs me back. I don't know when it happened, but he grew up. At six-feet tall and over two hundred pounds, my little boy has turned into a man.

"Are you coming?" I back away, holding my breath, and wait for Marco's answer.

He looks to Caleb and back to me before answering. "I'm going."

"Yes!" Mackenzie squeals and runs to her brother to give him a hug.

"So, you left to get your phone fixed and came back with Marco. How did that happen? And you never texted me back. I was worried."

Caleb looks at me sheepishly. "I haven't gotten it fixed, yet." He looks down at his watch. "Why don't we all go to dinner and I'll drop it off to get fixed while we're out."

I should question why he hasn't gotten it fixed and where he's been all day, but something tells me, whatever he was doing is the reason our son is home for the holidays, so I let it go, thankful to have my family together.

"Sounds good. How about I see if anybody else wants to join us?"

"Oh! Can we invite Kayla and Bentley, so Chloe and Faith can go? And Liz, so Lilly can go?" Mackenzie asks excitedly.

"Actually," Caleb says, "How about we just do dinner, the four of us? We'll see everybody at the cabin soon enough."

"Okay." I smile, liking the sound of that.

"Fine." Mackenzie frowns.

We get to the mall to drop off Caleb's phone and the guy says it'll be ready in about an hour. "Why don't we eat at the food court?" I suggest, and everyone agrees.

We get to the food court and Caleb and Mackenzie take off to the pizza place, while Marco and I go to our favorite sushi place.

"How have you been?" We're waiting in the long line to place our order and I figure I'll take advantage of the few minutes we have alone.

"I'm good, Mom. Just busy training. How are you? How's the clinic and the rec center?"

"Everything is great. I just miss you, Marco. I thought when you left almost two years ago, you would come home." Traitor tears fall before I can stop them. "I'm sorry. I don't know why I'm so emotional."

Marco envelops me in a hug. "Don't cry, Mom. I miss you so much. I'm sorry I've been gone."

"Is it something I did?"

He looks at me incredulously. "Are you crazy? You're the best mom I could ever ask for. I just needed to get away, find my own place in the world. I promise to start visiting more. You didn't do anything wrong."

"Okay, but when you left you—"

"Marco?"

Marco and I turn to the female voice who called his name. Bella is standing there with Tristan, Ashley's son, and for some reason she looks almost upset to see Marco.

When Marco doesn't say anything, she asks, "Are you going to Breckenridge?" Her voice sounds cold—detached. I never asked Marco if he kept in touch with Bella and Tristan after he left, but the look she's giving him doesn't look the way two old friends should look when running into each other after not seeing each other for so long.

For many years, despite the six-year age gap, the three of them were inseparable in and out of the gym. That was until Marco started high school. It made sense that a teenager wouldn't really want to hang out with kids six years younger, but the way Bella is looking at him, you would think something bad happened between them.

Marco just stands there, staring at her, so I answer. "Yes, he's coming. He surprised us for the holidays. When's the last time you guys saw each other?" I don't ask the question to anyone in particular, but Bella answers. "Probably like over a year ago…"

"Um, Mom. The line is moving," Marco points out.

I glance at Bella and she looks hurt. "Okay, well, I guess I'll see you guys on the plane tomorrow."

"Okay, honey. And we'll see you in a few days, Tristan."

"Bye, Hayley."

Bella and Tristan both wave goodbye and walk away.

"What was that about?" I glare at Marco. Something is going on.

"What was what about?" He shrugs nonchalantly.

"Oh, Marco, don't give me that crap. I've been around Bella for most of her life. Did you two have a fight?"

"I don't want to talk about it." He gives me a look that reminds me so much of Caleb. I nod in understanding, but I fully plan to get to the bottom of this. *Is she the reason why he's staying away?*

We place our orders and I try to jog my memory of anything that could have happened around the time Marco left. But she said over a year ago. That would mean they saw each other when he came back that one time to visit...

"Mom." I look at Marco, holding both our boxes of sushi.

"Oh, sorry." I take my box and pay the cashier.

"Mom, drop it, please." My kid knows me too well.

Kaden

"MASON! FOCUS!" I THROW A PUNCH TO HIS STOMACH AND he dodges it but just barely, his eyes finally coming back to mine.

"I am focusing! But damn, all these women that want a piece of me. How can I completely ignore that?" The kid waggles his eyebrows.

"If you don't focus, you'll lose your next fight and then the ladies won't want any piece of you."

"I'm focusing!" He looks to the left of me and I know damn well his ass isn't focusing. I throw another punch to his stomach, this time connecting a little too hard, but fuck! The kid is pissing me off.

Mason doubles over, more from not expecting it and less from it hurting. "Fuck! Kaden!"

"That's not very nice." I look to the left of me, following the sexy voice, and see my wife walking toward me. Then I look back at Mason. *Was this fool staring at my wife?*

Ashley's dressed like a fucking sin, in a blood red sweater dress with a big black belt wrapped around her middle. It's a business dress I've seen her wear before, but every time I see it, I wonder who in their right mind felt it was okay for a business woman to dress like that. Men wear suits. Suits which cover our entire body. Her dress isn't too short or too tight. It's just perfect. It accentuates all her amazing curves that I want to run my hands all over. Her ensemble is complete with a pair of high as fuck black heels that make me want to strip the dress off my wife and fuck her in only those heels.

Ashley only wears this dress for one reason, to get men's attention and money, which means she must have come from a meeting with potential donors.

"Be nice to Mason, Kaden." Ashley leans over the

ropes and gives me a soft kiss that only leaves me wanting more. "Mason, have you thought about whether you'll be joining us for the holidays? The gym will be closed and we would love to have you."

Mason is an up and coming fighter I took on a couple years ago. When he moved here, he had just turned eighteen and Marco had decided to take off to California. Shortly after Mason started training here, Ashley and I learned Mason was homeless. We ended up taking him in and he's been sharing a room with Tristan.

"I just hate to impose on your family vacation," Mason admits.

"You said that last year, but this year I'm not letting you use that as an excuse. As a matter of fact, I am insisting you join us and I won't take no for an answer."

He considers this for a moment and he must realize it's better not to argue with Ashley because he says, "Well, if you insist."

"Good! Is Tristan around?" Ashley looks around

then spots him on the treadmills with Bella. "Oh! There he is. I'm going to go make sure he knows what time we're heading to your parents' place tomorrow. Can you grab dinner on your way home? I need to run by Liz's to grab the girls."

"Sure thing."

Ashley leans back over to give me a chaste kiss then walks away, her ass swaying. My wife might be ten years older since we married, but her body doesn't seem to have aged a damn bit.

I look over at Mason and follow his gaze...right to my wife's ass. "Focus!" I yell. He just chuckles and says, "What? You have to know your wife is a MILF."

I throw a punch to his face and he blocks. "Fuck! I'm just kidding." His hands come up, palms out, in surrender.

"You wanna be thrown out on your ass? Make another comment about my wife. Now focus!"

"Okay, okay." Mason chuckles some more. "I'm

focusing. Damn, I'm sorry. She's too old for me anyway." We go back to sparring. "I have my eye on someone, though."

"Are we sparring or gossiping?"

"Sparring."

"Then more punching and less talking."

"Hey!" Cooper walks into the gym. "How's it going?" Mason and I stop sparring so I can walk over to Cooper to talk to him.

"It's going. Weren't you just here Saturday?"

"Yeah, I was here trying to keep all the crazy stalker girls from getting into the gym. I just wanted to see how it's going before we leave tomorrow. Has the place calmed down?"

"Yeah, it seems to have. The gym will be closed for a couple weeks anyway, so it will give the girls time to calm down over Mason's win."

"Remember when Marco won his first UFC fight?" We laugh. Las Vegas is a busy city and put a UFC training camp in the middle of it with a couple young guys who have made it in the UFC and you will get chaos.

"Yeah, he had no idea what to do with all that attention. Mason, on the other hand, loves it."

We hear Bella laughing and turn to watch Mason speeding up her treadmill making her laugh harder.

"Mason, would you stop?!" Bella smacks his chest and slows it back down bringing it to a stop. "Tristan, you ready to go?"

"Sure." Tristan brings his treadmill to a stop then gets off, grabbing a towel and wiping his face.

"I can't believe Bella was accepted to college out of state and she's actually going," Cooper says, continuing to watch his daughter.

"She's going to Cali for sure?" I ask.

"She says she is. Tristan's going as well, right?"

"Bella could go to Alaska and Tristan would follow her."

"She wants to go to San Diego for spring break to

look at apartments. She mentioned sharing a place with Tristan. I'm glad she'll have him there with her."

I look over at Cooper. There's so much I want to say, but I keep my mouth shut. Bella is his little girl and he's one of my best friends. If it were up to me, Tristan would go to school on the other side of the country. Don't get me wrong, Bella is a wonderful girl, and she's never been anything but good to Tristan. The problem is, while Bella sees Tristan as her best friend, Tristan sees her as more, and I don't think Bella will ever see him like that. One day she's going to fall in love and it will destroy Tristan. Unfortunately, as his dad, it's my job to just be there for him. He doesn't want to hear what I have to say when it comes to her, and if you ask him, he'll deny his feelings for her.

"You're okay with them sharing a place?" I ask.

"Of course, if she's going to leave the state, I'm glad she has Tristan with her. There's a UFC training facility in San Diego. I'm going to give them a call and make sure she's set up."

"Marco trains in San Diego, right?"

"Yeah, he lives about twenty minutes or so from the college campus."

"Hey Dad!" Bella jogs up to Cooper and gives him a kiss on his cheek. "I rode here with Tristan, mind giving me a ride home?"

"Sure thing, Princess."

"When do you guys arrive in Breckenridge?" Bella asks.

"Saturday. We're going to visit my parents first for a few days before we drive over."

"Cool! See you in a few days, Tris." Bella gives him a hug.

"What about me?" Mason smirks.

"What about you?" Bella puts her hand on her hip.

"Well, for one. Don't I get a hug, too? And I'll be joining them, so you'll see me as well." Mason winks and opens his arms for a hug, and Cooper smacks him upside his head.

"Don't even think about touching my daughter."

Tristan chuckles and shakes his head. "Let's go Mason. If you're catching a ride with me, I'm leaving. I need to shower and pack."

"All right...see ya soon, Bella," Mason calls from behind as he and Tristan leave the gym.

Ashley

"WHERE THE HECK ARE MY PILLS?" I LOOK INSIDE THE medicine cabinet, under the sink, and inside my makeup bag, again. This is the second time they've gone missing. I consider asking the girls, but if they didn't take them, I'll have to explain what the pills are for. Damn it! I'm going to have to call in another order. I check all the places they might be one last time, not finding them, then dial the pharmacy's number. Hopefully they can get me a prescription today. We're leaving tomorrow and if I can't get a replacement today, Kaden and I will have to use condoms. Ugh! The bitching that will ensue on his end. After speaking with the tech, she lets me know I can pick up the pills in an hour.

"Morgan! Emma! Come here, please," I call to the

girls down the hall.

"Yeah, Mom?" Emma answers for them.

"I need to go by the pharmacy to pick up a prescription. Nobody's home, so you two will need to come with me."

"Oh my God! We're ten years old. When will we be old enough to stay home?" Emma whines.

"Not until you're at least thirteen. Sorry. Let's go." I grab my purse and keys and the girls follow behind complaining about not being treated like an adult. I stifle my laugh. They have no idea what being an adult even means.

As we're getting into my SUV, Tristan and Mason pull up.

"Hey, Mom, where're you going?"

"I need to run to the pharmacy, but you have perfect timing because your sisters want to stay home. Let your dad know I'll be home in a few minutes."

Just as I'm about to get in my car, Kaden pulls up

and gets out of the car carrying bags of food.

"Where are you going?" he asks.

"Hey baby." I give him a quick kiss. "I need to run to the pharmacy. I lost a prescription that I need before we leave."

"Everything okay, Mom?" Tristan asks, concern etched in his voice.

"Yep, everything's fine."

"Tristan, grab these bags of food and go ahead and get the table set up. Girls, go with your brother and Mason." Kaden hands the bags over to Tristan.

"Why don't you come inside and eat and I can run to the pharmacy later?" Kaden doesn't make eye contact with me. *Hmm...*

Moving closer to Kaden, I ask, "Don't you want to know what I'm getting at the pharmacy?"

He continues to look everywhere besides at me, so I gently move his chin toward me. "Kaden?"

"Whatever it is, it can wait. Let's go eat dinner

with the kids." He grabs my hand, tugging me up the driveway. *Oh. Hell. No!*

"Kaden..." He ignores me. "Kaden, stop!" When he still ignores me, I pull on his hand. "Kaden Scott! Tell me you didn't do what I think you did...Twice!"

He slowly turns around. "Okay, I won't tell you." And now I'm fuming.

"You took my birth control? What the hell is the matter with you?"

"I want another baby." He says it so calmly, shrugging like he just told me he wants chicken fried rice with his Chinese order.

"Kaden!" I glare at him. "We talked about this. I'm almost forty years old and you're forty-five. We are not having any more babies. Our house is filled to the max."

"By the time you have the baby, Tristan will be moved out. The baby can take his spot."

I laugh at his ridiculousness. "Mason and Tristan are sharing a room. The room will still be filled."

"Then we can buy a bigger house." He shrugs so nonchalantly I have to hold myself back from punching him.

"I love our home. What's going on?" I take his hand, threading our fingers together.

"Nothing," he huffs out, and I hold back my laughter at his immaturity.

"Kade, talk to me." I give him a small kiss on his chin then another one on his neck. "Please talk to me."

"Fine. Yes, Tristan is moving out, and Morgan and Emma are ten going on twenty-five. They don't even need me anymore, and soon they'll move out and the house will be empty."

"Oh, baby." I wrap my arms around his neck, giving him a soft kiss. "Our home will never be empty. Sure, Tristan is moving out to go to college, but we have eight more years with the girls, and even once they leave, they'll be back. Whether to visit or to move back after college. One day they'll get married and they'll bring their loved ones with them. And think about once they have kids of their own."

"Stop. I don't want to think about them getting married or having kids. I want them to go back to being babies again." He pouts, and I have to kiss his lips again.

"I know, sweetie. But that's not going to happen. We just have to spend the time we have with them and make the most out of it. You know"—I give him a kiss, this time with my tongue—"once the house is empty, we'll be able to have sex anywhere we want."

This gets his attention. "Oh yeah? Like where?"

"Hmm...like in the kitchen. The living room. On the picnic table. On the stairs. And we can be as loud as we want."

Kaden chuckles. "You're the loud one, not me." *Yeah, okay.*

"Mom, Dad! C'mon! The food is getting cold," Morgan yells out the front door.

"Coming," I yell back.

"Oh, you will be...tonight," Kaden whispers in my ear.

"Not until I pick up my pills, I won't be." I shoot him a glare.

"I'll get them for you. They're in my glove box."

I smack his arm. "I knew your ass took them! Don't do that shit again."

"Fine." He pouts.

He runs to his car to grab my packet of pills, then we join everyone for dinner.

"We're leaving at seven in the morning." I remind everyone. "Grandma wants us there for breakfast. We're going to visit for three days with my parents, then after we go to Breckenridge, we'll spend New Year's with Grandma and Grandpa Scott before we come home. Please make sure you pack everything you need...phone chargers, toiletries, clothes."

"Mason, are you going?" Emma asks.

"I sure am. You know what that means, right?"

"What?" she asks, forking noodles into her mouth.

"We can train in the mountains. Jogging, hiking. It's going to be a blast."

"Ugh!" Morgan's face scrunches up in displeasure. "That defeats the purpose of vacationing."

"Morgan, be nice."

"Hey, Mom, did you still need to go to the pharmacy?" Tristan asks.

"No," Kaden says, sounding like a petulant child.

"I seem to have found my prescription after all." I smile at Kaden, and he pouts again.

"So, Tristan, I was talking to Cooper today and he's taking Bella to San Diego over spring break to look at places. Are you definitely wanting to room with Bella?"

"Yeah. Her rent will be covered by her scholarship. I got approved for tuition and books, but not for room or food, so I have to find a place like we talked about before."

Years ago, Kaden took money and put it into separate

accounts for the three kids. He said he wanted to make sure no matter what happens in life, they'd be able to go to college if they choose to. He didn't want them to have to struggle between working and going to school.

"Are you still planning to major in athletic training?" Kaden asks Tristan.

"Yeah, either that or sport's management. I've been considering maybe becoming a sport's agent one day. I don't know." While Tristan loves fighting and training, he isn't as dedicated to being a part of the UFC as Bella is.

"You can major in anything you choose to and you don't have to decide now," I tell him. "I got my degree in elementary education and look what I ended up doing, running a recreational center."

"Your mom's right, Tristan. All we want you to do is focus on school. We never told you this, but we put money aside for you guys for college. As long as you keep your grades up, the account we set up will continue to cover your rent, food, car insurance, cell phone, and anything else you need to get through school."

"Seriously?" Tristan looks from Kaden to me.

"Seriously."

"I don't want to go to college," Morgan announces.

"What do you want to do?" Kaden asks.

"I want to be a fashion designer."

"Then you'll need to attend a fashion institute."

"What's that?"

"It's just like college, where they teach you all about fashion. How about after dinner we look it up and I'll show you?"

"Okay! Cool!"

We all finish dinner, and while the boys clean up, Kaden shows Morgan all her options for fashion design. I grab my iPad and pull up the current book I'm reading hoping to get a few pages in.

"Hey Morgan, Emma, want to go get ice cream?" Tristan asks.

"Yesss!"

"Go and get your shoes on." Both girls run to their bedrooms.

"You joining, Mason?" Tristan asks, grabbing his keys from the hook.

"Sure thing. Maybe we should call and invite Bella." Mason waggles his eyebrows and Tristan shakes his head.

"Just leave her alone, bro."

"Why? I've given you two years and you haven't staked a claim on her. If you've changed your mind, say the word and I'll leave her alone."

"It's not like that with us. She's my best friend."

"So, you've been friend-zoned. You can change that if you want to..."

Tristan looks over at me, realizing they're having this conversation in front of me. "Just drop it, man. Let's go."

Mason chuckles. "You got it."

"Want us to bring you back anything?" Emma asks

as they all stampede to the door.

"No thank you, sweetie. Don't be too long, though. We have an early morning ahead of us."

"Okay, Mom."

The door closes behind them and I click back on my iPad.

"You hear that?" Kaden whispers.

"No, hear what?"

"Silence...a quiet house. Maybe we don't have to wait eight years to have sex all over the house."

"They're only going for ice cream. We hardly have time to do it all over the house."

"I'm confident we can knock out at least two of those places you mentioned." Kaden closes the gap between us and grabs my hands pulling me up against him, my book already forgotten.

"Oh yeah? Which places should we knock out?"

"Hmmm..." He taps his chin. "The picnic table would be a great place to start."

"You're crazy!"

"Crazy about you." Kaden pulls me out the backdoor, then grabbing my hips, lifts me and sets me on the picnic table, my feet resting on the bench seat.

"I'm sorry, Ash." Kaden gives me a small smile.

"For what?"

"For trying to get you pregnant without talking to you. It was a shitty thing to do."

"Yeah, it was. Don't do it again." I pull on his shirt and he falls forward against me, his hands landing on the table on either side of me.

"How about we just play pretend?" I murmur.

"Mmm...." Kaden places kisses on my cheek, along my jaw, on my lips. "I like to play with you."

His lips go back to mine, his tongue seeking entrance. I quickly unbutton my blouse, exposing my bra as Kaden devours my mouth, his kisses getting harder. Rougher. I can feel the heat pooling between my legs.

"Kaden..." I moan his name against his lips, needing

more, and of course, my husband knows exactly what I need.

Moving his lips downward, he trails kisses across my collarbone, over my shoulder, ending at the swell of my breasts.

"Damn, baby." Kaden's eyes fill with lust. He unbuttons the top of my dress, exposing my bra then kisses the top of each of my breasts. Unbuttoning a few more buttons, he pulls the cups of my bra down with his teeth, and my cleavage spills out. Taking one nipple into his mouth, then the other, he ravishes them. I love that even after all these years, my husband still wants me like a horny teenager.

Grabbing his belt, I undo it, then unbutton his jeans, pulling the fly down, and push his jeans and briefs to his ankles. I stroke his dick while he continues to give my breasts his undivided attention.

"Lie back, baby," he murmurs. I squeeze his dick, not wanting to let it go. "You'll have it soon. Lie back." He chuckles.

Reluctantly, I let go of his dick and do as he says, lying back onto my elbows so I can still see Kaden. He gives me a smirk, knowing I want to watch whatever it is he's about to do to me.

His rough hands start at my calves and slowly he runs his hands up my legs until he reaches the apex of my thighs.

"Lift up." I lift my butt and he pushes my dress up, exposing my panties. He bends down and kisses my mound through my panties. Goose bumps cover my skin.

"Lift up again." This time he pulls my panties down. The chill in the air hits me and I shiver.

Kaden's face disappears and seconds later his fingers spread my lips and his tongue runs up my slit. I sit up a little higher so I can watch and the sight of Kaden's face between my legs sends sparks straight to my core. I'll never get enough of this man.

"Play with those nipples, baby," he demands, his

mouth up against my pussy. I lie back all the way, close my eyes, and does as he says, enjoying the feel of his tongue on my clit. He inserts a finger, and then another, and a few seconds later, he's fingering me deep. It's only been a few days since I've gotten off, but it's long enough that I'm already squirming with pleasure about to explode.

"C'mon baby," Kaden encourages. He slips another finger in me, making me feel full as his tongue massaging circles on my hardened nub.

"I-I'm close," I call out.

"Give it to me, baby. C'mon."

His tongue licks harder, his fingers fuck me deeper, and within seconds, fireworks are going off behind my eyelids as my orgasm shoots through me.

"Fuck, yes," Kaden murmurs. I sit up on my elbows in time to see Kaden lifting his shirt to wipe his mouth, his perfect six-pack of abs peeking out. Then he leans down over me to give me a kiss. Even though he's wiped his mouth, I can still taste myself on his lips.

"Come here, Ash." Kaden takes my hand in his, helping me off the picnic table and then walking us over to the side.

"Bend over, baby." Doing as he says, I bend over the side of the table and Kaden pushes my dress back up to my waist. "Damn, Ash. In your heels, you're the perfect height for me to fuck you like this." He rubs circles over the globes of my ass then spreads my cheeks apart. With one hand, he guides his dick into me from behind, grabbing my hair with his other hand.

"Fuck, baby. You feel so good." He slowly pushes into me until he bottoms out.

He's just sitting there, teasing me, not moving. "Kaden, I need you to fuck me."

Without saying a word, he wraps his hand around my hair—so tight, it pulls my head back—and then starts to fuck me.

"Harder!" I beg.

He thrusts into me harder, his dick hitting deep inside of me over and over again.

"Yes. Yes. Yes," I chant, my words spurring Kaden on. He pounds into me, and with my breasts still spilling out of my bra, my nipples rub against the wood, stimulating me even more. A few thrusts later and I'm coming all over Kaden's dick, my body shaking and my legs turning to jelly.

"Oh. Fuck. Ash!" Kaden pumps into me a few more times before finding his own release. We stand there for a minute catching our breathes, Kaden's dick still inside of me.

"Hey," he murmurs, tugging gently on my hair. I tilt my head to the side and he kisses me passionately.

"Mom! Dad!"

"Oh shit!" I push Kaden back at the sound of the kids calling our names, forgetting his jeans are around his ankles. He stumbles back and lands on his ass.

"Jesus!"

"Sorry!" I whisper, quickly putting my bra back in place and buttoning up my top before pulling the bottom of my dress back down. Kaden pulls up his briefs and jeans but stays sitting down.

"There you guys are!" All four of the kids come out the back door. Luckily, we're both fully clothed except...

Oh shit! I spot my panties just to the left of Kaden. I try to tell him with my eyes, but he's oblivious.

"What are you guys doing outside?" Emma questions.

"Why are you sitting in the grass, Dad?" Morgan adds.

Mason smirks.

Tristan's eyebrows furrow.

I pray nobody notices my panties lying in the grass.

"Your dad and I were just out here..."

"Talking," Kaden finishes for me.

Mason walks over next to Kaden and steps on my panties then looks at me, laughter evident in his eyes.

"Let's go inside, girls," Tristan suggests, grabbing

them by their shoulders. Once they're turned around, Mason chuckles, then with his foot, kicks my panties into Kaden's lap.

"When I grow up, I want to be you," he says to Kaden, his chuckle turning into full-blown laughter. He walks back inside the house, his laughter still going strong.

"That was close," Kaden says, shaking his head as he stuffs my panties into his pocket.

"But so freaking worth it." I give him a wink.

Bella

WE'RE THE FIRST TO GET ON THE PLANE. MY MOM AND DAD grab a couch together and Nathan sits next to them begging to play gin rummy for the millionth time. The kid is obsessed with card games. Lilly finds a spot near my parents and opens her book to read. I grab a seat and get comfortable with my electronics and headphones. I choose a playlist to listen to on my phone while I search videos of previous UFC fights on my iPad.

I feel him before I see him, and it scares me because the last thing I want is for him to have this effect on me. After everything that has happened, I promised myself I would never let Marco Michaels affect me in any way ever again. Luckily, he doesn't sit next to me, not that I expected him to. He'd rather just mess with me from a distance. Without trying to make it obvious, I peek up to see where he's sitting and lock eyes with him.

And he smirks at me. *Fucking smirks.*

Marco

I STEP ON THE PLANE AND IMMEDIATELY, MY EYES FIND HER.

It's not intentional. I've spent half my life aware of her. I spot her sitting in a seat by herself in the corner, earbuds in her ears, probably watching old UFC videos. The plane is huge and seats twenty people easily. I could sit anywhere, but where do I sit? Right across from her. Why?

Because I'm fucked up like that.

Cooper

THE PLANE RIDE WAS SHORT BUT FILLED WITH CHAOS. Bentley rented one plane for all of us, and when I looked around, it made me laugh at how many of *us* there are now, and that's minus Kaden and his family, who are coming on a separate plane after they visit with Ashley's parents first.

Once we land, we check-in to grab our rental vehicles then we all head to the resort. While Bentley and Kaden both own a place here, Caleb and I haven't taken the plunge. Normally we rent a place, but since Bentley's parents aren't coming this year, we've decided to stay at their place. Maybe this year, I'll find a place I like enough to want to buy, or maybe I'll find a place in California since my daughter has decided she's going to be stubborn and move there.

Bentley's parents' place has four bedrooms with a guesthouse out back they built recently. Liz and I will share a room, Caleb and Hayley will get their own room, Nathan will have his own, and the three girls will share a room. Bentley said Marco can stay in the guesthouse out back if he'd like so he has his own space.

Everybody piles into the house and goes their separate way, hauling their luggage into their assigned rooms. I'm hoping this week I'll get to spend some time with Bella. My days are dwindling down until she leaves for California and I need to make the most of it. After unpacking my luggage, I head back down to watch some TV.

"So, what did you get Liz for Christmas?" Caleb asks. We're sitting on the couch watching Sports Center while the women make a list of groceries we need to pick up.

"Huh?"

"Liz...Christmas gift..." Caleb looks at me like I'm stupid. "You got her a gift, right?"

"Shit! I completely forgot to buy her a gift." How the hell did this happen? I've never forgotten to get her a gift. I can tell you how this happened. I was so stressed over waiting on Bella's college acceptance letters, my mind spaced out. Exchanging gifts has always been a big deal with Liz and me. It started the first weekend I met her almost twenty years ago. When we went our separate ways I left gifts for her to open every day she was still at the hotel. It's never been about the money. It's always been about the thought. First, it was gift cards for her to buy the books she loves. Then a necklace with a pair of boxing gloves. The entire Batman DVD collection. Her favorite dessert. Over the years, I've bought her charm bracelets, customized ornaments, the kids and I have made her gifts, and I have planned romantic getaways as well as family vacations. But this year...Fuck! I can't believe I didn't purchase or plan anything.

Caleb chuckles. "Bro, you're fucked. You better find a way to go into town and buy her a gift."

"Buy who a gift?" Marco sits on the couch next to us.

"Cooper forgot to buy Liz a Christmas gift."

Marco laughs. "That sucks. I'm so glad I don't have a girlfriend I have to buy shit for."

"You just wait. One day you'll be in this same situation. Keep laughing."

"Fuck that. Have you seen the family I come from? My bloodlines are tainted. I'll never subject a woman to that shit, let alone procreate."

"You are *not* your biological parents. Don't say shit like that," Caleb says. Marco and Caleb both come from shitty backgrounds. The two of them meeting was the best thing that could have happened to them. Well, aside from them meeting Hayley. She's the best thing for both of them.

Just then, the women and kids all come walking into the room.

"Everything okay?" Liz asks. The sudden tension in the room must be obvious.

"Everything's all good. How about I go into town to get the groceries?" *And buy you a present...*

"Oh! Well actually, I was going to go. I was hoping to pick up a tree so we can decorate it and put all the presents underneath. You can stay here and check out the slopes."

Caleb chuckles, coughing to hide it, and I make a mental note to punch him later.

Marco smirks then stands and stretches. "The slopes are looking really good right about now."

"I can grab a tree while I'm out. Just give me the list." I stand and grab the keys from the table.

"I would rather pick it out so I know it's the one I want," Liz argues, putting her hand out for the keys.

"You know what would be real neat? If we cut down our own tree this year! We could have the perfect tree," Hayley says.

"Yes! Can we?" Lilly and Mackenzie jump up and down.

"I can help cut it down," Nathan adds.

"I'll call Kayla and see if they want to join," Liz says.

"All right. Everyone grab their jackets and meet at the vehicles," Caleb announces. I count the days in my head. After today, there's three days until Christmas, which means I have two and a half days to find a way to leave on my own to go in search of a Christmas present for my wife.

"Can I stay here?" Bella asks. "I'm not feeling well."

"What's wrong?" Liz walks over to Bella and feels her forehead.

"It's probably just something I ate. I'm just going to lie down for a little bit."

"Okay, sweetie. Text or call if you need anything."

"You know what...I think I'll join in on this tree searching excursion," Marco says.

We all pile into the vehicles minus Bella and head to

the tree farm.

Bentley

WE GET TO THE TREE FARM AND I TAKE RYAN'S HAND IN mine while the girls go in search of a tree. Kayla decided to stay back and spend some time with her mom.

"Okay, little man, you ready to pick out a Christmas tree?" Ryan just looks at me. I wonder if he knows what Christmas is. I make a mental note to see if the resort has a Santa Claus we can go see. We usually go to the mall every year, but with the girls getting older, they find it to be silly. I need to remember all these things now that we have another little one in the house.

After about thirty minutes of everyone pointing at several trees, we've decided on the two trees we're going to cut down.

"Dad! Can you help us? Cooper said we have to cut

down the tree for our house!" Faith calls to me, and Cooper laughs.

"All right." I bend down to speak to Ryan. "I'm going to help them cut the tree down. I want you to stay right here, okay?"

"I'll keep an eye on him. Is this the famous Ryan I've heard about?" Marco smiles down at Ryan.

"It is. Ryan, this is Marco, he's Chloe's brother."

"Nice to meet you little guy." Marco lifts his hand to give Ryan a high five, but Ryan only stares. Marco puts his hand down, then kneels in front of Ryan to talk to him.

"I'm going to help them. I'll be right back."

I jog over to the girls who are holding the bow saw in their hands trying to cut the tree down. They look absolutely adorable, but they aren't even making a dent in the trunk.

"Coop, are you picking on my little girls?" I joke. The girls hand over the saw, and after putting on the gloves the tree farm loaned everyone, I start sawing the tree trunk. Thankfully, we picked smaller trees so within a few minutes I'm half way through. Cooper is sawing the other tree and he's almost done. The tree is already tipping to the side.

"Everyone move," he yells, and the tree tips all the way over hitting the ground, snow flying up into the air. I finish sawing our tree and it hits the ground shortly after his.

"All right! Let's load them up onto the tractor trailer so they can bring them up."

The kids grab parts of the trees and start dragging. The adults watch for a second, all of us silently laughing at the fact that the kids aren't dragging the trees anywhere.

"Some help would be nice," Faith grumbles.

After the trees are loaded, I look around for Ryan. When I don't see him, I start to freak out. Nothing is scarier than losing a child, but add a mute child to the scenario, and it's downright terrifying.

"Have you seen Ryan?" I start asking. Everyone shakes their heads and starts looking around them.

"He was just here." Now I'm panicking.

"Ryan!" I yell, hoping he'll answer. Everyone is searching. My heart is pounding, my palms are sweaty. I need to find my son. Right now.

"Ryan, where are you?" I shout pointlessly, but hoping if he hears me, he will at least find me.

"Bentley, calm down." Marco appears from a woodsy area. Shit! While panicking, I forgot Marco was with Ryan! I take a second to calm myself because I don't want Ryan to see me upset.

"He's right here." Ryan comes out from behind Marco and I grab him and pick him up, giving him a hug. I don't know what I would do if something ever happened to him.

"I couldn't find him and my mind went blank. I completely forgot you were keeping an eye on him." I hug Ryan tighter.

"He's fine. We were having a great conversation. Weren't we, Ry-man?"

Ryan nods. I chuckle.

"Oh yeah, what did you guys talk about?" I ask, going along with the pretend conversation they had.

"Ryan said his favorite food is pizza. I told him we could order some when we get back to the house because it's also my favorite food."

"He did, did he? You want pizza, little man?"

Ryan nods.

"Anything else?"

"He said he likes the snow. I promised him we would make a snowman. Isn't that right?"

Ryan nods again, a ghost of a smile gracing his lips.

"Okay, then. Pizza and a snowman. I think we can handle that."

We walk back to where the others are. "Oh, thank goodness!" Liz places her hands on either side of Ryan's face. "We thought you got lost." She gives him a kiss on his forehead.

"It's my fault. Marco said he would keep an eye on him and I completely forgot."

"All right, everybody ready to head back?" Caleb asks.

"Hey Liz, why don't you and the girls head back with Bentley since he has the extra room and I'll run by the store," Cooper suggests.

"Or you can go with him?" Liz says. "I know everything we need to get."

Caleb laughs softly and Marco chuckles.

"What's going on with them?" I whisper to Marco.

"Cooper forgot to get Liz a Christmas gift."

"Oh goodness." Hayley shakes her head.

"What's wrong?" Caleb asks.

"Liz forgot as well." We all laugh.

"Should we tell them?" I ask.

"Hell no, this will be too much fun to watch." Caleb

chuckles.

Liz

"I WOULDN'T WANT YOU GETTING LOST." COOPER SMILES wide and I know his ass is up to something. Is it possible he knows I completely forgot to buy him a Christmas gift? If he does, damn him for making this difficult on me on purpose. After all the years we've been together, the one time I forget, he's going to make sure to rub it in.

"I'm sure I can handle it."

"Hey guys," Marco says. "It would probably be best if we all just go because I need to grab a few things as well."

I hope my glare shoots a dagger straight through his throat! Marco picks up on my glaring and physically recoils. Good! Too bad it's too late.

"Fine, let's all go together!" I start stalking back to the car.

The guys finish tying the trees onto the top of the vehicles then we all take off to the store. Once we've picked up groceries as well as ornaments and lights to decorate the trees with, we all go back to our houses.

"Bella! We're home." I check the rooms but don't see her anywhere.

"I thought she wasn't feeling well." Cooper hands me a note from Bella letting us know she went for a walk to the resort.

"I don't think it's her health that's the problem." I eye Marco bringing the groceries in. "I have a feeling it's her heart."

Cooper follows my gaze to Marco but doesn't catch on. Sometimes men can be so obtuse. "I'm going to go look for her. I'd like to spend some time with her," Cooper says, putting back on his gloves and jacket.

"Okay." I give him a kiss. "Have fun."

As soon as Cooper walks out the door, a thought occurs to me.

"Hayley! I need a favor."

She's walking down the hallway, frowning at her phone. "What's up?"

"Everything okay?"

"Yep!" She shoves her phone into her back pocket and I make a mental note to ask her what's going on later.

"Copper left. I need to go to town to get his gift. Can you keep an eye on Nathan and Lilly for me?"

Hayley laughs. *Bitch!* "Of course! But what do I say if he gets back before you do?"

"Just tell him I forgot something at the store!" I rush around the house grabbing my jacket, cell phone, and keys. "Thanks!"

Hayley

"LIZ RUNNING OUT TO BUY COOPER A GIFT?" MARCO GRABS some items from the bag and puts them into the fridge.

"Yeah." I giggle, thinking about Liz running out of the house in a rush. "Ever since their first Christmas when she surprised him with a trip to Disney, they've been determined to one up each other every year."

"Ha! Yeah, I remember a few years ago when they both bought each other a cruise!"

"Oh my God, yes! And it was for the same cruise and during the same week."

"That was hilarious! The look on their faces was priceless." Marco shakes his head, laughing. "And this year they completely forgot to buy a gift."

"Yep."

"It will be funny to see who pulls it off and what the gift is."

After we finish putting the groceries away, I'm about to head back to the living room, when Marco asks if I would like a cup of coffee.

"Sure, but only if we can have one together on the back porch."

"Deal."

He makes us both a cup and we take them out onto the porch. There's a swinging bench that overlooks the resort and it's breathtaking this time of year. The way the mountains are covered in snow creates such a serene backdrop.

"How have you been?" I sit on the bench next to Marco.

"I'm good." He takes a sip of his coffee without giving me anything more.

"Oh no, I need more than that. I finally have you in front of me." I give him a side-eye.

Marco lets out a sigh. "I'm really good, I promise. You know I'm living my dream. I'm fighting and winning. I'm making money doing what I love. I can't imagine doing anything else with my life."

"I'm so proud of you, Marco. Any women in the picture?"

Marco gives me a side glance. "There's some."

"Any of them serious?"

Another sigh.

"Talk to me, sweetie."

"It's like I told dad, my bloodlines are tainted. I don't want serious. I don't want to get married and have kids." Even though I shouldn't be, I'm shocked by his admission. I thought the years of therapy he's attended along with Caleb and I providing a loving home would have trumped his past.

"You've never said anything like this before."

"You and Caleb saved me. He saved me from a shitty situation, from a druggy mom. You took me in and made me yours. I don't ever want to let you guys down."

"What?" I look at him stunned. "How would you let us down?"

"By not having a family. Not getting married. I used to hear you and your friends talk. About how you all can't wait to be grandmas one day. The wedding. Parties."

"Marco, as long as you're following your dreams, you could never let us down. Never. But your reasoning is crap."

"It's fact," he shoots back.

"So, Chloe is tainted?" Marco stays silent, knowing I have him. "Is she, Marco? Is Caleb tainted? Because you know what he went through."

"His stepmom did that shit to him. That's not blood."

"And his father turned a blind eye."

"I found my dad."

"What?" I'm shocked. Marco's father, who wasn't listed on his birth certificate, is dead according to what his mom used to tell him.

"I mean, I know he's dead, but I found his family. I hired a private investigator. Aunt Jenn knew his name and where he was from. She didn't want to tell me, but I begged."

"Why?"

"I needed to know. My biological mom was always a drug addict since as far back as I could remember, but she used to be a good mom before Chloe's dad died. I don't remember a whole lot. I remember certain things, but I have no recollection of my dad. My aunt Jenn said my mom always struggled but was never into drugs until my dad came around."

I don't say anything, letting him tell me whatever he needs to say at his own pace.

"My dad was a huge drug dealer and had several families. I have half brothers and sisters all over the damn place. The PI found a couple of the women and they're all druggies like my mom was. He destroyed every one of those women. So, while Chloe has our biological mom in her genes, I have that man in me. The one who fed women drugs and destroyed their lives. At least Chloe's dad wasn't a piece-of-shit like mine. Sure, he wasn't the best role model, but he didn't feed my mom drugs and devastate everything in his wake like my dad did."

"Oh, Marco. You're so wrong about genetics. You might share eye or hair color, but who your parents are doesn't mean that's who you are. You don't do drugs and you don't destroy anyone around you."

"I was selling them at like twelve years old. I'm just as bad as he was. And then with Bella..." Marco trails off, and I have a feeling he didn't mean to let that part slip.

"Stop it." I turn toward my son and look at him, for the first time realizing even after all these years, he's still so broken. "You did what you had to do to survive. There's a damn difference. If you don't want to have kids or get married, fine! But don't you ever compare yourself to anybody else, especially to that man. You are you. You are loving and caring. You are passionate and determined. You are *my* son and I love you. You complete me in so many ways.

"And your father, the man who has raised you. He was so lost when he met you. And you came into his life and saved him. So, don't you ever say you are tainted. You are not a bad person, and you are ours."

"I've done other bad shit."

"Bella?" I ask, referring to his previous statement.

Marco looks at me and for a moment I think he's going to open up to me, but instead he shuts down. "It doesn't even matter. I fucked up and I can never take it back."

"Whatever you did, I want you to know I would never judge you and neither would your dad." Marco flinches when I mention his dad but doesn't say anything.

"Marco, I need to ask. Did something happen with Bella?"

His eyes widen for a brief second before his elbows fall to his knees, his hands scrubbing over his face. He looks at me like he wants to talk to me, and I silently beg him to, but instead he says, "No."

We both sit in silence for a few minutes, drinking our coffees.

"Ryan is a cute kid," Marco says, changing the subject.

"Yeah, it breaks Bentley and Kayla's heart that he won't speak, but hopefully he will soon."

"What do you mean? He speaks." Marco's brows furrow together.

"He's learning sign language, so he communicates, but he hasn't spoken since the day they got him. His parents were young and into drugs. His mom committed suicide and his dad forfeited his rights. He was neglected."

Marco shakes his head, looking perplexed. "Umm... Mom...Ryan speaks. He spoke to me."

Kayla

"WOW! YOU GUYS, THIS TREE IS BEAUTIFUL!" BENTLEY JUST got back with the girls and Ryan from handpicking a Christmas tree. He set it up in the stand, and the girls put water in it. It's big and fluffy and I love it. I also love that this is the first tree with Ryan and my mom here.

"Thank you for taking the kids. My mom and I had a nice talk."

"Any time, babe." Bentley grabs my hips and pulls me into him for a kiss. It's supposed to be a quick kiss but nothing with Bentley is ever quick. His lips touch mine and his tongue enters, and like always, when my husband puts his hands and mouth on me, I melt like snow into a puddle of water at his mercy.

"Oh God! You guys!"

"Seriously! Will it ever stop?"

The girls start complaining and I can't help but laugh against Bentley's mouth.

"Do your parents do this a lot?" my mom asks through her laughter.

"All the freaking time," Faith huffs.

"It's so gross and should be against the law." I can hear Chloe's eyes rolling to the top of her head.

Bentley gives me one more kiss then releases me. "Later," he promises.

There's a knock on the door and both girls run to get it.

"Marco!" Chloe gives her brother a hug.

"Jeez Chloe, you're acting like you didn't just see me a little bit ago." Marco laughs but picks her up giving her a bear hug.

"I know, but I need to see you a lot now because once you go back to California you won't come back for a long time." Chloe pouts. Caleb and Hayley have taken her with them when they've gone to visit Marco, but it's not the same thing as her brother living in the same city as her.

"I'm sorry, Chloe. I'll try to visit more. Now that you're getting older, maybe your parents will let you visit me. I live on the beach so I can even teach you to surf."

"Mom, can I?" Chloe starts jumping up and down in excitement.

"Maybe we can all take a trip out there. You know, I used to be a pretty good surfer."

"Pretty good? Woman, you won championships before you moved to the northwest," Bentley points out.

"Damn, Kayla. I didn't know you could surf. Can Liz?" Marco asks.

"Ha! No way! She used to sit on the beach and read her books while I surfed. Gosh, it's been so long. We should plan a trip to the beach soon."

"My place is small, but it's surrounded by hotels.

You guys should definitely come over," Marco suggests.

"Sounds good! So, what brings you guys by?" I look at Hayley who appears to be nervous.

"My mom said Ryan doesn't speak."

"He doesn't. But he will."

"He does speak, though. Where is he?" He looks around for Ryan.

Bentley whips his head to me in shock when he hears what Marco said. "Wait a second. Marco, when you were keeping an eye on him for me and you relayed your conversation with him to me, were you being serious?"

"What conversation? When was Marco watching Ryan?" I'm confused.

"When we went to cut the tree down. Marco kept an eye on Ryan for me so he wouldn't go near the trees or wander off. He was telling me about Ryan's favorite food and what he thought about the snow, but I thought he was just playing around." Bentley turns to Marco. "Were you just playing around?" Bentley's voice is rough with emotion.

"No, I didn't even know Ryan doesn't talk. He told me that stuff himself. I swear." Marco looks nervous.

"Marco, Ryan has never spoken. His biological father said he spoke at times, so we know he can speak, but he hasn't since we got him."

"Where is he now?" Marco looks around some more for Ryan.

"He's in his room taking a nap."

"Kayla, go grab him," Bentley insists.

"What if Marco goes up there and records it? That way Ryan doesn't feel overwhelmed," Hayley suggests.

"Facetime! He can do a Facetime chat so we can hear it live," Faith exclaims.

"Yeah, I can do that...but..."

"What?"

"I don't want you guys to be disappointed if he doesn't talk again."

"Marco, I can't even believe he talked in the first

place. This gives us such hope. If he doesn't then he doesn't. But maybe he trusts you, and he will." I shrug. "It's worth a shot."

"Okay, I'll go up there. Chloe, Facetime me so it's live."

"Okay." She pulls her phone out of her back pocket.

Marco

I WALK INTO RYAN'S ROOM, MY PHONE BURNING IN MY hand knowing everybody downstairs can see and hear everything. I've never been this nervous before. I know Ryan spoke to me—there's no way I was imagining it—but now that I know he doesn't usually speak I'm worried he won't do it again and everyone will think I'm fucking nuts, or that I lied, or be disappointed.

My phone vibrates and I quickly look at it and see it's Bella. I hit decline. I'll deal with that later...or not. Ryan is lying in his bed with his eyes closed. When I sit, the bed dips a little and his eyes open.

"Hey Ry-man." I set the phone down next to me so everyone can hear and maybe see. Ryan looks at me but doesn't say anything. He blinks a few times, waking up, and I give him a minute. After he sits up, I start talking to him.

"So, I was thinking maybe you and I could go build that snowman. What do you think?" Ryan nods. Shit, I need to get him to speak.

"And afterward we can get pizza." He nods again. I need to ask a question that requires him to answer with words.

"What kind of pizza do you like?" Ryan blinks a couple times and I hold my breath. Then he leans toward me and whispers, "The one with the red circles on top." He speaks the words slowly, his eyes going wide.

"Pepperoni. I like that one too."

He nods.

"Who should we have go with us to build the snowman?"

Silence.

Then he whispers, "Faith...and Chloe."

"Okay, what about your mom and dad?"

He nods and smiles.

"Can you do me a favor?"

Ryan nods.

"When we go downstairs, can you tell your mom that you want pizza?" Ryan's eyes widen. He doesn't answer one way or another.

"All right. Let's go down and get everybody, so we can make a snowman."

Ryan scoots off the bed and takes my hand in his. I pocket my phone and we head down the stairs back to everyone.

Bentley

HIS VOICE. WE HEARD IT. IT'S SOFT AND BARELY THERE, BUT it was his voice. Tears fill my eyes and Kayla hugs me around the waist as we stare at Chloe's phone. We can't see Ryan or Marco, but we stare at the screen anyway as the words come through the speaker.

"Oh, my God. Bentley. He spoke." Kayla cries next to me as we take in the significance of this moment. Ryan and Marco come down the stairs and we quickly compose ourselves, wiping the tears from our eyes so Ryan won't get scared.

Ryan walks up to us with his hand still in Marco's. "Go ahead, Ry. Tell your mom what kind of pizza you want so she can order it." Marco is soft-spoken and kneeling next to Ryan. Kayla kneels as well and gives

Ryan a small smile.

Ryan looks over to Marco and Marco nods in encouragement. "Pizza with red circles." It's only four words, spoken so softly you would miss them if the room wasn't quiet, but fuck if they aren't my new favorite words.

Kayla takes in a deep breath to keep her composure. I know what she's thinking. If Ryan sees her crying, he'll assume the worst, so instead she smiles big. "We'll definitely get you pizza with red circles. What would you like to drink?" She's hoping to keep him talking. I can feel everyone watching and waiting with bated breath.

Ryan looks to Marco. I have no idea why he's attached himself to Marco, but for whatever reason he has. It's clear in the way he looks at him, he trusts him, and while it hurts that he opened up to him after only knowing him for thirty seconds, I will be forever grateful.

Marco nods and smiles encouraging him.

"Milk, please." His please comes out like peas and I turn my head for a second to wipe the tears.

"Pizza with red circles and milk. You got it." She goes to stand, but Ryan starts talking to her again, freezing her in place.

"And...melon."

"Melon?" She clarifies.

Ryan nods. "The red one." *Watermelon.*

"Okay, we'll get you some watermelon."

Ryan nods...and smiles. For the first time since he's moved in with us, he gives us a toothy grin and it just about brings me to my knees.

"Liz went into town to get...something she forgot. I'll call her to pick up watermelon," Hayley says.

"All right, Ry-man. You ready to build that snowman?" Marco asks Ryan.

Ryan's eye light up and he nods, but then he says, "Yes."

Best. Day. Ever.

Cooper

I TAKE OFF TO FIND BELLA ON FOOT. SINCE SHE MUST BE ON foot, I figured how far could she have possibly gotten. I don't have to look far before I find her up in the Breckenridge ski resort. She's curled up in a reading chair with her iPad in her lap reading a book with a hot coffee in her hand. She reminds me so much of Liz at times. It shouldn't surprise me, though. She raised her for the first four years of her life on her own. The bond they share is unbreakable.

From the moment I met my princess, we formed our own bond, one that has survived all the stages of my little girl growing up. It wasn't until the last year or so that our bond has started to fray and my biggest fear is that when she leaves for college that thin thread will break and not be able to be sewn back together. My goal is to prevent that from happening but in order to accomplish this, I need to be prepared to hear anything she has to say whether I like it or not.

And let's face it, at my daughter's age, there's a good chance whatever comes out of her mouth will be shit I'm not going to like.

"Mind if I join you?" I stand over Bella, waiting for her permission to join her. She clicks off her iPad and sets it next to her, giving me a small smile.

"Of course. Where is everyone?"

"They're at the house. I wanted to spend some time with you. Talk to you."

"You can talk to me any time." Her nose scrunches up in confusion just like her mother's does.

I sit down in the reading chair next to her. "I feel like you're slipping out of my grip."

"I'm just going to college like one state over. I thought we already talked about this." She frowns.

"It's more than that. We used to talk every day while training. Now it feels like you've already moved even though you're still right in front of me."

She sighs softly. "I guess I just feel lost right now."

"Why?"

"I'm going to college because you want me to, but all I want to do is train and fight."

I know she hates that we've given her an ultimatum. Go to college or she needs to get a job to support herself. She's not eighteen yet, so she can't fight in the UFC and even then, it'll be years before she's making any kind of money. She's got to start fighting and winning first.

"We just want more for you, Bella. I didn't go to college. Yeah, I inherited my dad's gyms and did well in the UFC, but that's not always the norm. And your mom, she was pregnant at eighteen and struggled in college, juggling her school work and having a baby, but still graduated."

"Do you think she regrets having me?"

"No way. That's not what I meant. You're the best thing that ever happened to us, aside from your siblings. I just meant that we want things to be easier for you. We've worked hard so we can give you whatever it is you want."

"But I don't want college. I don't think it's for me, but you're giving me no choice."

"Are you going away to California because you're mad at me?"

"No." She shakes her head.

"Why don't you stay here and go to a state college and train with me?"

"I—I just need to be on my own. I need some space."

"What if we get you a place here?"

"Dad, I love you, but I need some breathing room. I need to be able to grow and learn and make mistakes away from here."

"What kind of mistakes, Bella?" She bows her head, and I know she isn't going to tell me. Hell, maybe she doesn't even know what mistakes, yet. All I can do at this point is be there for her even when she doesn't know she needs me.

"Hey," I say. "Your mom and I are here for you. No matter what. Whatever mistakes you think you need to make, fine. But we're here. All we want for you is to pave a path for your future. Fighting can come first, but you need a backup plan. You need a college degree."

"I know, Dad. And I'm doing it your way." I want to tell her she doesn't have to go to college. I want to tell her whatever it is she wants to hear that will bring my little girl back to me, but the hardest part of being a parent is doing the things you feel are best for your children even if it hurts you to do so. And I really feel it's best for Bella to go to college while training. All it takes is one injury and she'll need to find another career. It happens to athletes every damn day. Hopefully one day she'll understand where we're coming from.

"I love you, Bella."

"I love you too, Dad."

"Want to do some snowboarding? There's still a couple hours of light left."

"That sounds like fun. Let's do it.

"Yeah?"

"Yeah."

We spend the next couple hours snowboarding. Bella might look like her mom and love books like her, but athletically, she is most definitely my kid. Fighting, skiing, snowboarding, it doesn't matter what it is, she picks it up quickly and excels at it.

We get back to the house a few hours later and I notice our rental car is gone. We walk inside and Caleb and Hayley are cuddled up on the couch together.

"Where are the kids?"

"Playing in the snow in the backyard."

"Liz?" Hayley and Caleb exchange a glance.

"She mentioned something about needing to drive out..."

"How long ago?"

Caleb looks at his watch. "Damn, must have been a couple hours ago."

I text her to make sure she hasn't gotten lost.

Me: You okay?

I don't get a response right away and that starts to worry me. The snow has been coming down the last couple hours. What if she got stuck somewhere?

After a few minutes, I send the text again and get no response. Then I notice the message turns green, which means Liz's phone is either off or she has no service.

"Have you spoken to her since she left?"

"No, but I did text her asking to pick up watermelon for Ryan and she never responded."

"Caleb, would you mind me borrowing your car? I'm worried about Liz."

"Of course, but I'm sure she's fine." He pulls the keys from his pocket and throws them my way.

Hayley's phone chimes and she stands up, walking

out of the room while frowning down at her phone.

"Hey, Hayley, is that Liz?" I yell after her.

"No, sorry," she calls back.

"Everything okay with her?" I nod toward where Hayley just was.

Caleb shakes his head. "I don't know, man. I'm trying really hard not to assume anything but something is up." He stares at the ceiling for a second then says, "Look, I shouldn't tell you this, but I know you're worried about Liz and her being gone. She went into town to buy you a gift."

"What?"

"She forgot to buy you a gift, too." He smirks. "I'm sure she's fine. She's just in town shopping."

"I'm going to drive around just in case. It's not like her to have her phone off."

Bella

AFTER MY DAD AND I RETURN TO THE CABIN FROM snowboarding, I head out back to join the kids playing in the snow. While, I'm excited to be heading to California to school, I'll miss my siblings and parents like crazy. When I get out there, the kids are running back inside saying they're hungry, and I see Marco walking in the opposite direction. He must be going back to the guesthouse he's staying in behind Bentley's parents' place. Instead of making myself known, I walk back inside to join my family.

Seeing Marco is hard, which sucks because there was a time when seeing Marco made my day. Then...stuff happened. Emotions were involved, feelings were hurt, and instead of dealing with it, Marco chose not to. What

I want is to knock on his door and make him deal...and maybe I'll do just that. But not now. Because I'm a damn chicken.

Liz

I DON'T KNOW HOW MANY TIMES WE'VE VISITED COLORADO over the years and every single time, Cooper has said the same thing when I'm driving.

Liz, no matter what, you do not ever swerve for an animal in the road.

And every time he would say it, I would roll my eyes. I mean, c'mon, what idiot would swerve on the snowy, slippery road and risk their own life just to make sure the animal running across the road doesn't get hit.

I can hear his voice in my head, like he's saying it right now.

Liz, no matter what, you do not ever swerve for an animal in the road.

And his words totally make sense...until you're

driving along the snowy, slippery road and a cute deer with her cute babies come running across the street. I swear I heard his words...

Liz, no matter what, you do not ever swerve for an animal in the road.

But then I imagined the poor innocent mama deer and her poor innocent babies getting hit by my big SUV and them dying and it being all my fault, so I ignored Cooper's words...and swerved, which is why right now I'm sitting on the side of the road, in the snow bank, with my front two wheels stuck in a ditch.

I try to put the SUV in reverse, and for a second, I think my vehicle is going to back up over the side of the ditch...until the bottom of my car hits the ground and bottoms out. I can hear the tires spinning, getting deeper, and know I'm stuck.

Wanting to keep in the warmth as long as possible, I stay in the car and grab my phone from my purse to call Cooper. It's going to suck to have to tell him what happened, but I don't really have a choice. Pressing the circle on the bottom of my iPhone to open it up, a bright red battery sign mocks me on the screen. Damn it! The phone is dead. No wonder I was shopping for so long without being bothered. Whoops!

And I would like to say after all this, I bought my husband the perfect present that is going to make this entire shitty situation worth it, but sadly I didn't. You would think the longer you know someone, the easier it would be to buy them a gift...Wrong! I swear there wasn't a single thing in that entire shopping plaza to buy him.

Now, don't get me wrong, I'm not stupid. I bought him a gift. With Christmas only a few days away, I had to get something! So, I got him a wallet. I bought the man a wallet! Don't get me wrong, there's nothing wrong with a wallet as a gift, but it's so impersonal. It's so not us. I have a strong feeling this year will be the year Cooper outdoes me in the gift department.

After sitting here for a few minutes, I check around to see if maybe there's a car charger. Of course there isn't, so I decide to get out of the vehicle and go in search of a phone. Opening the car door, I put one foot out and step right into a huge pile of snow. Eww! Snow! Hence the snow bank...My poor Uggs might be really cute and sold during winter, but they are *not* meant to be worn while plowing through real snow. Ugh!

I get completely out of the vehicle, ankle deep in the wet, sloshy, snow, and look around. I wasn't even paying attention to where I am. The built-in GPS tells me where to go and I follow it. I look to the left and there's road. I look to the right and guess what's there? Road! No houses, no stores, nothing! Just road. *Great!*

I turn the vehicle back on and press the home button, which is the address of the cabin we're staying in.

"To proceed to the route, please make a U-turn when possible."

What the heck! The GPS must have messed up from

the lack of service. When I click to zoom in on the road, it shows I'm on a back road called Boreas Pass and I'm eleven miles from the resort. Well, there's no point in just sitting here. Maybe somebody will drive by and stop so I can use their cell phone.

I lock the SUV and start walking in the direction the GPS told me to head in. Even with a snow jacket and gloves on, I am freezing. It's not snowing and the sun is shining, but holy shit the air is a frigid bitch.

A few minutes later, I see a car driving up. I wave my hands in the air hoping they'll stop but no such luck. They just keep on driving. *Real nice! Just remember karma is a bitch, people!*

I'm not sure how long I've been walking, but I'm starting to get worried. Eleven miles shouldn't be too bad, right? Cooper and Bella run close to that daily. But at the same time, it's cold and snowing and I am not dressed for this frigid hike.

I see another car approaching, and just like the one

other time, I wave my arms in the air hoping this person will take mercy on me and stop, and to my luck the vehicle does stop! Please don't let it be a serial killer!

And thank God, it's not, it's my husband! Only when he gets out of the vehicle, the look on his face almost makes me wish it were a serial killer who stopped.

"I saw our rental car back there! Why the fuck are you walking in the wrong direction from our cabin?"

Whoops!

Cooper

I'M DRIVING TOWARD THE SHOPPING PLAZA WHEN THE GPS tells me to make a slight turn onto Boreas Pass. When I look at the dashboard, it shows there's an accident on the main road so the GPS is having me take an alternate route. My heart picks up and I pray Liz isn't anywhere near the accident. I'm driving not even two minutes when I come across our rental vehicle on the side of the road stuck in a snow bank.

Jumping out of the car, I run to the driver side door only to find the vehicle empty. I look around me and yell, "Liz!" but she doesn't answer me. I glance back toward where I came from and wonder if I somehow missed her. I jump back into the SUV and start driving back, my mind starting to race with horrible thoughts.

What if she's injured? What if someone hit her while she was walking? What if someone took her and killed her?

My horrid thoughts keep progressing and I have to turn my mind off. She's fine. I just need to find her. I drive back to the main road but don't see her. It doesn't make any sense. I turn the vehicle back around and drive past our vehicle. About two miles down, I see a tiny woman walking along the snowbank. I slow down and her arms start waving frantically. Why the hell is Liz walking in the wrong direction?

I pull over, confused and angry, and get out of the SUV, slamming the door behind me.

"I saw our rental car back there! Why the fuck are you walking in the wrong direction from our cabin?"

Liz looks to the left then to the right and then glances back at me confused. I just shake my head. My fucking wife has no sense of direction whatsoever.

Thankful she's alive and uninjured, I wrap her up in my arms and kiss her hard.

"I was so worried, babe."

"I'm sorry. I swerved for a deer and her babies and ended up in a snow bank. My phone is dead and the GPS got messed up."

I have to bite my tongue. I've told her a million times not to swerve for animals. "C'mon, let's get back to the cabin and we can call for a tow truck to get the SUV out of the ditch."

We get back to the vehicle, but before I put the car in drive, Liz wraps her arms around me. "Thank you for saving me. I was starting to get so scared."

"Baby, I will always save you." Liz turns my face toward her and kisses me. At first, it's soft, but then it gets more aggressive, her emotions showing through. I reach over, without breaking our kiss, and grab the curves of her hips, bringing her onto my lap. Our kissing continues. Our tongues entwining with one another. When we break for air, her lips don't stop. She kisses my cheek, my jawline, then she moves to my neck.

"Cooper, I want you. Now." My cock stands at attention, realizing he's going to get to come out to play. Without thinking twice, I press the button to push the seat back, giving us room. Liz lifts her ass up, pulling her jeans down while I unzip mine, taking my cock out. It's a tight fit in the SUV, but nothing is going to stop me from getting inside my wife. Her shoes and pants go flying and I push mine down.

She sits back on my lap, her pussy grinding against my now hard shaft. Leaning down, she gives me a kiss over my heart then looks me right in my eyes and says, "I need you inside me."

Best. Wife. Ever.

Sticking a digit into her to make sure she's wet, I find she's dripping. She lifts her sexy ass up, and before I can push my cock into her warmth, she grabs my shaft and guides it in herself. As she comes down slowly, her head falls back, eyes closed, in pleasure. I grab her amble tits in my hands and roll her nipples between my fingers, eliciting a moan out of her.

Once I'm all the way in, she opens her eyes and smiles at me. *Fuck! I love this woman.* Taking one of her tits into my mouth, I suck on her puckered nipple then give the other one the same attention. Liz's hands come up landing on my shoulders, and then she lifts her ass up a few inches before coming back down, my cock hitting her deep. So fucking deep.

She starts off riding me slow, her tight pussy gripping my cock. My hands stay on her tits, massaging them, tweaking her nipples. The more her pussy adjusts to my cock, the faster she rides me. "Oh God! Cooper!"

Leaning closer to me, she brings her mouth to mine, kissing me with abandon as she rides my cock. I can feel her pussy grinding me as she finds the perfect spot to get herself off. Reaching down with one hand, I feel for her clit and am met with an, "Oh fuck!" when I find it. It's muffled, her lips still locked with mine.

Gathering her wetness, I start rubbing her clit. The

deeper I rub, the harder and faster she rides me, her moves growing more frantic. I know she's close when her legs tighten up and her movements get faster, even more crazy like she can't control herself. Her kisses become more intense, her mouth sucking on my tongue. A few more circles on her clit and she's climaxing all over my cock, choking the fuck out of it.

Her face falls to my shoulder and her body goes limp. Grabbing her hips, I take over, pounding into my wife from the bottom. Her pussy spasms around my cock from her orgasm and it creates a domino effect. A few seconds later and I'm coming deep inside of her warmth.

Needing a few minutes to come down from our high, neither of us moves, until...there's a knock on the window.

"Oh my God! Cooper!" Liz shrieks, attempting to cover herself. Luckily the windows are somewhat tinted, but I'm sure whoever is at the window can see our bodies enough to know what's going on. Reaching down with

Liz still on me, I grab her shirt and hand it to her to put on. Then I look around and see some napkins in the center console. Lifting her off my cock, gravity takes over and my cum drips down the inside of her leg. And holy shit, if that doesn't have me wanting round two. I quickly wipe it up the best I can with the napkins and set her in the passenger seat, handing her the napkins so she can finish cleaning herself up.

She wipes up quickly, pulling her panties and pants up, zipping and buttoning them. I use a napkin to wipe my cock and pull my briefs and jeans up. Once we're both decent, I roll down my window and come face to face with an officer. Thankfully, his badge reads Wildlife.

"Where was he when I was walking?" Liz huffs out.

"Officer," I say, nodding my head.

"Is everything okay here? I saw an abandoned vehicle a few miles down."

"My wife swerved for an animal"—I give her a side-eye—"and ended up in the snow bank. I found her walking."

"Well, I'm glad everything is okay. I can call for a tow truck if you'd like."

"That would be great. I don't think there's any damage. We just need to get it out of the snowbank."

The officer turns his back on us, walking to his truck, probably to radio someone to call for a tow truck.

"You wanna tell me why you drove out without me?" I already know the answer to this, but I want to see Liz squirm. She has no idea that we both forgot to buy each other gifts this year. Clearly, we're a match made in heaven.

Her shoulders rise and fall and she makes an annoyed huffing noise. "Fine! I forgot to buy you a Christmas present." She rolls her eyes, waiting for me to give her shit.

"I did too." I shrug.

Liz's head whips around to look at me. "You did?" Her smile widens.

"Yep, I did. That's why I was trying to run out without you earlier."

She shakes her head and laughs.

"I guess we're even."

"No way, crazy! You ran the SUV into a ditch. I saved you and gave you a damn good orgasm. I win. Merry Christmas."

Caleb

"ALL RIGHT! WHO'S GOING TO THE SLOPES?" I RUB MY HANDS together excitedly at finally getting a chance to do some snowboarding. We've been here for two days and only Cooper and Bella have hit the slopes so far. Cooper, Marco, Bella, and Chloe all raise their hands.

"You going, Bentley?"

"I looked it up and found out Santa is doing story-time at the resort for the kids. Kayla and I are going to bring Ryan to see him."

"Oh! I want to go!" Liz exclaims.

"Me too!" Faith says at the same time Mackenzie says she wants to go as well.

"Hayley?"

"I'm going with Santa." My wife hates skiing, so that

doesn't surprise me.

"Okay, let's split up and meet back here for dinner."

We head over to the resort, and after renting our equipment and putting it on, we take the lift toward a decent slope but one still easy enough for Chloe.

"Hundred bucks says I make it down this slope quicker than you do, Dad," Bella taunts. According to Cooper, Bella was kicking ass the other day.

"You don't even have a hundred bucks," Cooper scoffs.

"I don't need it because I'm going to win."

Marco chuckles, earning him a glare from Bella. "What? You want in? I bet I beat you as well."

Marco shakes his head, then says, "Okay, you're on."

The lift reaches the top and everyone lines up. "Hey Bella, when Marco and I beat you, where are you getting the money to pay us both?"

"Not happening, Pops!" Bella yells, taking off down the slope. Marco and Cooper both take off after her.

Bella

MARCO HAS BARELY LOOKED AT ME THIS TRIP LET ALONE spoken to me, so when he decides to get in on the bet, it's on like Donkey Kong. There's no way I'm letting his ass beat me. I take off with all the determination in the world to win. I'm avoiding the ramps I would usually try to hit to do some tricks, only focusing on making it down to the bottom first, and I think it's going to happen. I might have had a few second head-start but whatever.

Then, as I'm feeling confident, seeing the end near, Marco flies right by me carving the snow like the damn showoff he is and I know I'm screwed. I try to pick up speed by leaning forward and continuing to avoid anything but the straight away, but it's not happening.

When I make it to the bottom, he's standing to the side with a huge smug smirk on his face. I roll my eyes and look back up the hill for my dad. He's coming down and behind him is Caleb and Chloe.

"Guess I owe you a hundred dollars." My dad laughs. "Or should I just give it to Marco? Because by the look on both your faces, I'm guessing he beat you."

I huff in frustration and walk away, but before I can get far, Marco stops me and says, "Double or nothing, Belles?"

"You're on."

Ashley

"HELLO? WE'RE HERE!" AFTER DROPPING OUR STUFF OFF AT our house, where Tristan and Mason insisted on staying, saying they were both jetlagged, Kaden, the girls, and I went over to Bentley and Kayla's place. Kayla's mom answered and said everybody was at Bentley's parents' place so we headed over there to join everyone. It's Christmas eve and we've come from having dinner with Kaden's family.

"Ashley?" Kayla yells out. "Get in here!" Kaden closes the door behind us as the girls run upstairs to find the other kids, while Kaden and I join everyone else in the kitchen, where they're all drinking.

"What are we celebrating?" Kaden jokes, grabbing a beer from the fridge. Liz hands me a mixed drink straight from the blender.

"Well, it is Christmas Eve," Cooper says.

"And Ryan is finally talking!" Kayla gushes. "You should have seen him talking to Santa. I'll have to show you the video later."

"What? He's talking? That's amazing!" I give Kayla a hug.

"I don't know how Marco did it, but for some reason Ryan opened up to him and got him to talk. It's only small phrases and sometimes only one word answers, but for the last few days he's been talking."

"Where is he now?" I look around realizing there's only adults in the kitchen.

"He's asleep at the house. My mom had a headache so she offered to stay home with him. Marco put him to bed. I hope once the trip is over and Marco goes back to California, Ryan doesn't regress."

"Mom, I'm going to see Tristan! He texted and said they..." Bella enters the kitchen and sees us. "...arrived."

"I don't want you walking over there in the dark," Cooper says.

"He's meeting me half way. Bye!" Bella runs back out the way she came in.

The next hour is spent drinking and reminiscing. Everybody's drinking too much and we all know come tomorrow morning, we're going to regret it when the kids are up early and wanting to open their gifts, but for now we're enjoying ourselves.

"Biggest regret?" Liz asks.

"That's hard!" Kayla whines.

"Easy. Not giving you my number or getting yours," Cooper admits.

"Mine is not kissing Hayley back the night at the club," Caleb says.

"The night we played truth or dare?" I laugh. "That was hilarious! I completely forgot about that night. Now that I think about it, I never even got to get a dare!" I pout.

"Only you would be upset about not getting to participate in a teenage kissing game." Kaden rolls his eyes, taking a swig of his beer.

"You're just mad because you didn't get dared either." I laugh and take a sip of my very strong strawberry daiquiri.

"I wouldn't have needed to be dared to kiss you, Ash."

"Who says I would have wanted it to be you, anyway?" I stick my tongue out at him.

Everybody laughs like I just said the funniest thing, ever.

"What's so funny?"

"You," Hayley says. "It was so obvious how much you were pining after Kaden. If we could go back all those years and finish playing truth or dare, you'd be begging to kiss Kaden."

"That's not true!" I say defensively. "I wasn't pining after Kaden. There's a lot of other people I would have kissed that night."

"Yeah, like who?" Kaden asks incredulously.

"Like..." I think for a second, but my brain is fuzzy from all the liquor and I know better to name a man, so I say the first name that comes to mind. "Hayley! I would have rather kissed her than you that night. You were talking to all those women back then. At least I knew where her mouth had been." *Ha! Take that!*

"Now that's a kiss I would've loved to see!" Caleb raises his beer to Kaden who smirks and nods in agreement.

"So, you're saying you would've rather been dared to kiss Hayley than me that night at the club?" Kaden quirks a brow.

"Maybe." There's no way I'm backing down now.

"So, kiss her," he taunts.

What? "What?"

"Kiss her. Kiss Hayley. Right here. I dare you." Kaden grins, thinking I won't really do it. *Game on!*

"Fine."

"Wait? What?" Hayley suddenly realizes she's a part of all this. "I don't know..." Before she can finish her sentence, I close the space between us. With one hand holding my drink, I grab the back of her head with my other hand and bring our lips together.

The kiss is stiff at first, but the alcohol quickly kicks in, and seconds later, Hayley's tongue is seeking entrance. I part my lips, adding my tongue to the mix. Her lips are soft and gentle, unlike Kaden's strong and firm ones. The kiss isn't bad, but it's not Kaden. But I'll be damned if I tell Kaden that.

"Mom!"

"Oh my God!"

"Hot damn!"

Hayley and I pull apart and both turn to face the voices. Bella, Tristan, and Mason are all standing in the doorway.

Tristan's face looks sour.

Bella is shaking with laughter.

Mason is smiling ear to ear.

"Did you finally get tired of making out with Dad after all these years?" Tristan asks, his face still showing his disgust.

"No, but he dared me!" I point out, and yes, I'm aware I sound very much like the teenagers who just caught us kissing.

"I'm assuming this is one of those moments when we should do as you guys say and not as you do?" Bella smirks.

And everybody bursts out in laughter.

Hayley

"WHAT DID I MISS?" MARCO COMES WALKING THROUGH THE back door into the kitchen.

"Nothing," I say quickly as Caleb says, "Your mom making out with Ashley."

I shoot Caleb a glare and he waggles his eyebrows.

"Someone should have videoed that shit," Mason says.

Marco looks around the room like we've all lost our mind until his eyes land on Bella, then something in his face changes. I'm not sure what it is but call it a mother's intuition, something serious is going on between the two of them, and whatever it is, it can't be good, especially with the way he spoke about how badly he messed up the other day.

Unfortunately, I'm too drunk to have this conversation with Marco now, and if I'm honest that kiss with Ashley got me slightly turned on. Not for her, but for my husband.

"I'm ready for bed," I inform Caleb, who gives me a knowing grin.

"Sounds good to me."

Everybody agrees it's time to call it a night, and I vaguely hear everyone saying goodnight and goodbye, but I'm too focused on getting upstairs and into the room with my husband.

Once we get inside, he locks the door behind us.

"Damn, Hayles. I didn't think you had it in you to kiss another woman like that." Caleb grabs me by my hips and picks me up, carrying me to the bathroom and setting me on top of the counter.

"Did it turn you on to see me kiss Ashley?"

"Fuck yeah, it did. I saw your tongue go into her mouth. You were totally into that shit, babe." Caleb smirks then peels off his shirt, revealing his perfect abs. We've been together for almost twelve years and I swear I'm even more attracted to him than I was all those years ago.

"Arms up." I comply, lifting my arms up over my head, and Caleb lifts my shirt up, then reaches behind me, expertly unclasping my bra. Leaning in closer to me, Caleb gives me a kiss, his tongue wrapping around mine. I'm prepared for him to fuck me right here on the counter, but he backs up taking his warmth with him, and turns the bathtub water on, then dumps a bath bomb in to create bubbles.

"A bath?" I ask. "How romantic."

Caleb glares. "I can be romantic."

"I know you can. I'm just joking." I wrap my arms around him and bring his lips back to mine. For the next few minutes we make out like teenagers, our limbs entwined in one another. Once the tub in almost full, Caleb taps on my thighs. "Lift." I do, and he takes my panties and jeans off before stripping himself of his bottoms.

Picking me up, he carries me to the bathtub then sits against the back of the tub, placing me between his legs, my back to his front.

The water is hot and feels divine, warming me up from the chill of the outside Colorado winter. Caleb doesn't waste any time. Taking my loofah, he squirts body wash on it then starts to massage the soap onto my neck and shoulders. Everywhere he massages and rinses, he gives a kiss afterward, sending chills up my spine and down to my core.

I squirm a little and feel his hard length poke me in the butt, so I purposely wiggle to feel it against me. Caleb moves the loofah over my shoulders and to my breasts, massaging them. He stops at my nipples and gives them extra attention, causing me to squirm some more.

"Caleb." That's all I need to say for my husband to

know I need more. With his other hand, he spreads my legs open—the water sloshing around us—and sticks a single finger into me.

"Mmm...more," I moan. He pulls his finger out but immediately pushes it back in, adding two more to the mix, filling me. He starts to fingerfuck me, still massaging my breasts with the loofah. With his chin, he pushes my head to the side and suckles on the sensitive part of my neck. My body feels overstimulated from his touch. It's like there isn't a single part of me that isn't being pleasured by Caleb. My climax quickly approaches and I come hard all over his fingers.

Before I can even come down from my orgasm, he turns me around to face him, and places me on top of him, his dick entering me in one swift motion. With my legs feeling like jelly, it's hard to participate, but Caleb takes control, lifting me up and down. He leans forward, bringing our lips together in a searing kiss.

"Hayles, I need you to come again, baby. Massage

that clit."

Holding on to the side of the tub with one hand, my other hand comes down massaging the already sensitive nub. I'm so wet, even in the water I can feel how slick my arousal is.

"Caleb, I'm going to come." He picks up his rhythm, and the only sound that can be heard is our wet skin slapping against each other. It's all too much, and seconds later we're both coming.

We sit in the tub for a few minutes, our breathing heavy, coming down from our orgasmic highs, when my phone vibrates on the counter. We both look at it. Me, scared what it might contain but needing to know. Caleb, having no idea to even be scared for me.

"Hey." Caleb nudges me with his chin. "What's going on?"

I swallow thickly. "Nothing."

"Hayles, don't you dare lie to me. I've seen you check that phone a million times the last several days. Talk to me."

I sigh. "I went to the gynecologist a few weeks ago and they found a spot during my pap smear. My doctor thinks it could be cancer. So, she had me come back in and she did a colposcopy."

"What the hell is a colposcopy?"

"It's a procedure where the doctor checks my cervix and takes a piece to biopsy to see if I have cervical cancer."

"Hayley!" Caleb booms. "You've been going through this all on your own?"

"I didn't want to worry you if it was nothing."

Caleb wraps his arms around me tight. "When do you find out the results?"

"Any time now. That's why I've been checking my phone. The results will get uploaded to the patient portal."

Caleb grips my hips and lifts me off him, standing us both up. Then grabbing two towels, he wraps one around me and the other around him. He steps out of the tub first then helps me out.

I go to my phone and click on the mail icon.

"The results are in," I say nervously.

"Hayles, whatever the results are, we'll handle it."

I click on the email and log into the patient portal then click on the results. I read the results three times to make sure I'm reading them correctly.

"Negative."

"Negative?" Caleb repeats.

"It says the biopsy concluded I'm negative for cervical cancer."

"Jesus, Hayles." Caleb drops his head to the top of my own, and I wrap my arms around him, my face seeking comfort in his chest.

"I'm sorry, Caleb. I should have told you."

"Fuck, baby. I love you so damn much. I only knew of the possibly for thirty seconds and I felt sick to my stomach. I can't believe you kept this to yourself for weeks. Don't ever do that again."

"Okay," is all I can say. We stand like this for God knows how long and then Caleb backs up a little and looks at me with a serious look on his face. One I don't see often.

"What?"

Caleb shakes his head and graces me with a small smile. "I'm just so fucking happy. I never imagined my life would be like this and to think it could all be taken away from us at any minute... Fuck. You are my entire world. You, Marco, and Mackenzie. You guys complete me."

Bella

IT'S LATE—PROBABLY ALMOST MIDNIGHT ON CHRISTMAS eve—when everyone says goodnight. Like everyone else, I go to my room and lie down. Only, I can't make myself go to sleep. I can't stop thinking about Marco, and I wonder if this is my last chance to talk to him before I move to California. I know two people can live and train in the same city and avoid each other, but that's not what I want. Marco has been in my life for so long. The idea of going another year or more without us talking makes me sad.

Deciding to stop dwelling and obsessing, and just go to him so we can talk, I grab my cell phone and head out back, making sure I'm quiet, so I don't wake anyone up.

I get to the guest house and knock before I chicken

out. About a minute later Marco answers the door.

"Bella." One word. My name. Yet it has so many emotions behind it.

"So, about that bet..."

"You here to pay up?"

"I'm here to discuss payment options. Can I come in?"

Marco studies me for a moment. What he's looking for, I'm not sure, but whatever it is, he must find it, because he opens the door wider to allow me access.

Marco

THIS WOMAN IS GOING TO BE THE DEATH OF ME.

Kaden

"MERRY CHRISTMAS, GORGEOUS." I ROLL OVER IN BED TO face my beautiful wife. I can't imagine ever getting tired of seeing her lying next to me in the morning, her caramel colored hair splayed out across her pillow, her body tucked into mine like I'm her body pillow. It's Christmas morning and it's also the last Christmas we'll have together before Tristan moves out of the house, so it's bittersweet.

"Mmm...Morning...Merry Christmas." Ashley gives me a kiss that makes my cock twitch. But before I can get her under me, there's a knock on the door.

"Mom! Dad! Santa came." While I'm pretty sure the girls no longer believe in Santa, since there are so many kids among our group of friends, it's an unwritten rule

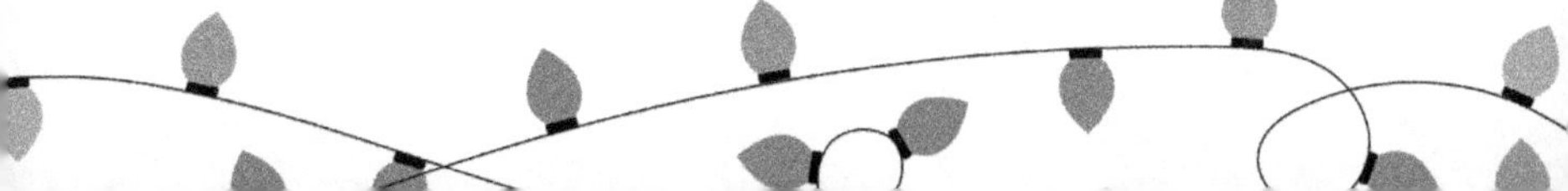

that it's always Santa who delivers the presents.

"Coming!" Ashley yells back to them.

"I wish," I mumble.

"Oh stop!" She smacks me in my chest and gets out of bed. I follow her out the door and down the stairs. We are opening presents from Santa as a family then everyone will be meeting at Bentley and Kayla's place to open presents together and have dinner.

The girls begin tearing through their gifts. Because they're younger, they have tons of shit. Coloring books, makeup, clothes, some board games.

Ashley grabs a thin box from the corner where we keep a small fake tree, which gets pulled out of the closet when we don't have time to get a real one. "Here's one of your gifts, sweetie." She hands the box to Tristan. "It's for you and Mason." Mason looks shocked. We don't know much about him or his past other than him not seeming to have any family. He won't discuss his past and we've accepted that.

"Here Mason, you open it," Tristan insists.

Mason takes the gift and unwraps it slowly. "Two tickets to New York?"

Tristan grabs them then looks in the box, pulling out a piece of paper. "A week in New York? Are you serious?" He looks back and forth between Ashley and me.

"Hell yeah!" Mason and Tristan fist bump. "When is it for?"

"It's for spring break. Bella is getting a ticket as well. We know you guys were talking about going to California to find an apartment but Cooper and I can find a place without going over there. We want you guys to enjoy your last spring break before you start college."

"Thanks, guys." Tristan and Mason both reach over and give Ashley and me a hug.

The girls open the rest of their gifts in record speed. Mason, of course, messes with the girls, telling them he's stealing their makeup. Tristan smiles but stays silent. I have a feeling he's thinking about the same thing I was earlier. This is his last Christmas before he moves out.

"You okay?" I bump him with my shoulder.

"Yeah, I'm going to miss them."

"You aren't moving across the world. And you know anytime you want to come home, you can. Speaking of which. Here's one of your other gifts. It's not really a gift so to speak, but well..."

I hand him a small box.

"It's from your mother and me."

Tristan opens the box and inside is a credit card and a pair of keys. He lifts the card and looks at me confused.

"The card is linked to the money we set up for you for college. We want you to go to college and focus on school. If you want to fly home, you purchase the flight. Whatever you need, this card will work. And if for whatever reason you don't feel California is working for you, you can always come home. The key is to your new Ford Raptor. I know you like your truck, but we want you to have something reliable." I get choked up on the last word.

Tristan looks me in my eyes. "I love you, Dad. Thank you."

One would think he's thanking me for the card and keys, but I know it's more than that. I might not be his father biologically, but Tristan is my damn kid just as much as his sisters are.

"No." I shake my head. "Thank you."

This kid has given me so much more than I could ever give him.

Marco

"MERRY CHRISTMAS." A SOFT, FEMININE VOICE WAKES ME from my sleep. Afraid to open my eyes, I lie still and pray this is a dream. It won't be the first time I've dreamt of her. Then I feel a delicate hand come up and run down my middle toward my dick and I know it's not a dream.

Grabbing the hand before it touches me, I count to three then open my eyes.

Yep...I'm fucked.

Bella

IT'S CHRISTMAS NIGHT AND EVERYONE IS TOGETHER AT Kayla and Bentley's house for dinner. Well, everyone except for Marco. He made up some ridiculous excuse and took off back to California. Caleb begged him to stay and fly out tomorrow, but he insisted he had to fly out today.

I look around me and feel so blessed. I was only four years old when I met my dad so I don't really remember it, but what I do remember is with him came an entire family. First it was the guys then came the women and kids. Over the years, it went from my mom, Aunt Kay, and me to an entire swarm of family.

I've never felt alone. I never had the opportunity to feel alone. Between my aunts and uncles, my siblings and pseudo cousins, and my best friend, Tristan, there's always someone around. But even with all these people here, surrounding me with their love—and there's got to be like twenty-five people here—for the first time I feel lonely. Like a piece of me is missing.

I can't explain it. It's like a hole in my heart...a rock in my stomach. It hurts and aches and it feels like even with all the love and laughter emitting off everyone in this room, it's still not enough.

But instead of dwelling on this weird feeling, I push it to the side. Like I said, I'm blessed. I don't have a right to complain and I sure as hell can't make someone want to be a part of my life.

I spot Tristan on the other side of the room and he shoots me a smile. It's crazy to think about the fact that in five months I'll be in San Diego at the University of California, and shortly after, Tristan will be joining me. While I'm not thrilled about going to college, I'm excited to start this new chapter of my life. I'm excited to kick up my UFC goals a notch. In two months, I'll be eighteen and I have every intention of making a name for myself in the UFC. I'm also looking forward to going to New York with Tristan and Mason. That trip will be epic.

"Penny for your thoughts?" I glance over and Tristan is now sitting next to me.

"We have the best family."

"Hell yeah, we do." He hands me a wrapped present. "Merry Christmas, Bella."

I take it from him. It's small, but thick and solid. I try to shake it, but it's heavy.

"Just open it." Tristan laughs.

I tear the wrapping paper off, finding a book inside. "Open it," Tristan encourages.

I open the thick cover and what I find inside knocks the breath out of me. It's a photo album. The first image is of my mom, Aunt Kay, and me when I was little. One in front of our old house, of my dad and me holding the Maleficent doll he bought me. Then there's one of Tristan and me on our first day of MMA classes with our toothy grins. There's one of the day my dad's name was added to my birth certificate and I had my last name changed to Cooper. I keep flipping the pages as hot tears begin to fall. There are so many pictures and they're in chronological order. Tristan and me at tournaments, ones of Marco and me sparring, at the aquarium when we were younger. Me holding Nathan when he was a baby. Lilly and me baking our dad a cake for his birthday.

The tears are coming down so heavily, I have to blink them away so I can see the photos.

"Tristan, this is beautiful."

"Your mom helped me make it. We've been through a lot together, Bella. But this isn't the end."

I look up at him and he gives me a soft smile.

"It's just the beginning."

The End!

About the Author

Reading is like breathing in, writing is like breathing out.– Pam Allyn

Nikki Ash resides in South Florida where she is an English teacher by day and a writer by night. When she's not writing, you can find her with a book in her hand. From the Boxcar Children, to Wuthering Heights, to the latest single parent romance, she has lived and breathed every type of book. While reading and writing are her passions, her two children are her entire world. You can probably find them at a Disney park before you would find them at home on the weekends!